The Runner and the Saint

Dave Duncan

Five Rivers Publishing
WWW.FIVERIVERSPUBLISHING.COM

Published by Five Rivers Publishing, 704 Queen Street, P.O. Box 293, Neustadt, ON N0G 2M0, Canada

www.fiveriverspublishing.com

The Runner and the Saint, Copyright © 2012 by Dave Duncan.

Edited by Dr. Robert Runté.

Cover Copyright © 2014 Jeff Minkevics.

Interior design and layout by Lorina Stephens.

Titles set in Monotype Corsiva, designed by Patricia Saunders at the Monotype Corporation.

Byline and headers set in Trajan Pro, designed in 1989 by Carol Twombly for Adobe, based on Roman square capitals.

Text set in Century Schoolbook, originally designed by Linn Boyd Benton in 1894 for American Type Founders.

All rights reserved. Without limiting the rights under copyright reserved above, no part of this publication may be reproduced, stored in or introduced into a retrieval system, or transmitted in any form or by any means (electronic, mechanical, photocopying, recording or otherwise), without the prior written permission of both the copyright owner and the publisher of the book.

Publisher's note: This book is a work of fiction. Names, characters, places and incidents either are the products of the author's imagination or are used fictitiously, and any resemblance to actual persons living or dead, events, or locales is entirely coincidental.

Published in Canada

Library and Archives Canada Cataloguing in Publication

Duncan, Dave, 1933-, author

The runner and the saint / Dave Duncan.

Issued in print and electronic formats.

ISBN 978-1-927400-53-1 (pbk.).--ISBN 978-1-927400-54-8 (epub)

I. Title.

PS8557.U5373R846 2014   C813'.54   C2013-908177-1 C2013-908178-X

Contents

Prologue	4
Chapter 1	15
Chapter 2	20
Chapter 3	30
Chapter 4	45
Chapter 5	52
Chapter 6	60
Chapter 7	67
Chapter 8	77
Chapter 9	87
Chapter 10	92
Chapter 11	103
Reality Check	107
About the Author	108
Books by Five Rivers	109

Prologue

Ivor had been running for two days. He was tired all over, from the leathery soles of his bare feet to the coarse black thatch on his head. And he was about to meet the king.

Although he and Chief Runner Ninian had made frequent stops to eat, drink, and catch their breath, sleep had been a rarity. They must have slept at times, but Ivor couldn't remember when or where. Now, in the slow gloaming of a summer evening, they had arrived at their destination, the royal palace of Scone, and he had no interest in looking at anything. What he saw seemed much like the mormaor's fort at Stiegle—a stone wall on a hilltop with thatched cottages inside. In a grey blur, he followed Ninian up to the entrance. Shivering as his sweat dried, he leaned against the wall while Ninian shouted to the guard to open the gate. The two runners stood there obediently when guards came out to inspect them, examine their silver belt buckles engraved with running horses, and grudgingly admit them.

They were escorted inside by swordsmen along alleys

between the cottages. A man opened a door and proclaimed, "Runners from Earl Malcolm, Mormaor of the West, sire." And they were ushered into the presence of His Grace Constantine II, King of the Scots and Picts, Lord of Alba.

At that point Ivor did wake up some. The room was small, lit by sweet-smelling beeswax candles. It had tapestries on the walls and was furnished with a table and some stools. There was also a chair, and a surprisingly young man standing in front of it. He wore a fine linen gown and a moustache, but no beard, and he looked tired. *He* looked tired? At the moment Ivor was the world expert on tired, but this must be the king, because Ninian was bowing.

"Ninian of Whisht!" the king exclaimed. "Welcome! Prepare meat and drink for these men. So, Ninian, what have you brought me this time?"

"This, sire." Ninian aimed a thumb at Ivor. "His name is Ivor of Glenbroch, and he is the youngest and newest of the mormaor's runners."

So it was Ivor's turn to bow. He knew that the reason Ninian had brought him along was to show him the way and present him at court, so he would be admitted whenever he came in future, but he hated being displayed like a hunting trophy. And now King Constantine himself was looking him up and down. Mostly up. But he did not make jokes about ship's masts or bulrushes.

"Welcome, Ivor of Glenbroch." He had a soft, musical voice. "Glenbroch...? Ah, yes. The housecarls there recently deposed their thane and promoted Tanist Tasgall."

"And the new tanist they elected, sire," Ninian said, "is Angus of Bracken, who is Ivor's eldest brother."

"Indeed?" The king looked impressed. "I have heard of Angus of Bracken! So you must have been Ivor of Bracken before you left the glen to run for Malcolm?"

"Aye, Your Grace," Ivor said.

"And you were named for your father, the great Ivor of Bracken! You are sprung from a noble line, Ivor."

To which Ivor could only mutter, "Thank you, Your Grace," and hope he wasn't blushing under his mask of dust and dried sweat.

"How old are you?" The king seemed genuinely interested.

"Sixteen, Your Grace."

"And you managed to keep up with Ninian all the way here from Stiegle? That was well done!"

"Not so, sire," Ninian said. "I managed to keep up with him, but only just. Oh, those legs of his! I feel a hundred years old. I may never run again."

The king laughed. "You are a lying churl, Ninian of Whist! So what did *you* bring me, Ivor son of Ivor?"

Oh! "This, sire." Ivor hastily unlaced his satchel to pull out the scroll he had carried for the last two days. He was annoyed that he and Ninian had been sent to deliver a written report. Any stupid horseman could have brought that.

King Constantine accepted the scroll with a sigh. "Then you fine gentlemen are free to go and attend to your hunger and thirst, and to enjoy some well-earned rest, while I must summon some gossipy cleric to read all this to me and tell me what your master has to say. I shall send for you both in the morning. God grant you a good night."

The runners bowed and departed.

Ivor and Ninian gorged on roast pork, onions, and small beer—anyone who drank water without some beer in it would soon die of belly fever. They spent the night in the king's hall, on a floor so packed with housecarls that they barely had room to turn over. The snoring had already begun when they got there and probably it roared like thunder all night long, but Ivor of Glenbroch heard none of it.

▶▼◀

Roosters announced the dawn, cows lowed to be milked, and a bell tolled. Another hot day lay ahead, another day of frantic preparation for war.

"So what did you think of the king?" Ninian asked as he and Ivor sat up and cautiously stretched, counting their aches and inspecting their feet for blisters.

"He's very, um, polite," Ivor said, then found a better word, "Gracious."

"That's why they call him His Grace, I suppose. He's a good king. Men are proud to serve him."

He was very different from Malcolm, Mormaor of Stiegle, who was somehow,... harder. Ivor was proud to serve Malcolm, but Constantine had impressed him too, in their few moments together.

The two runners barely had time to rinse off at a trough and gulp down some bread and honey before a page came to take them back to the king's presence. Kings worked long hours, it seemed. He was in the same room as before, staring out the window, but he swung around with a smile when they entered. Ivor guessed what was about to happen and his heart sank.

"Ninian and Ivor! Malcolm sent some questions that need answers right away. My own runners are all out on missions. Does either of you feel fit enough to run back to Stiegle right away?"

Two voices said, "Aye, sire!" simultaneously.

"You're certain?" Constantine asked. "Normally I would never ask a man to do this so soon."

It occurred to Ivor that Malcolm might have asked that question once, but not twice like that. He joined Ninian in insisting he was ready and able. He was *not* going to be bested at running, not even by Malcolm's captain of runners. He had beaten Ninian in a race on the day they met, which was the reason the mormaor had hired him, and Ninian had never asked for a rematch. Word of the newbie's strength had spread quickly, for none of Malcolm's other runners had ever challenged him.

"Very well," the king said. "This will have to be verbal, though." That implied that it was too secret to write down, which would have meant passing the information through the ears of a clerical scribe in Scone and the mouth of a clerical reader in Stiegle. The only people who could read and write were either priests or monks, and both whispered to bishops. Bishops liked to meddle in the affairs of kings. Runners used their memories and were sworn to secrecy. Being a runner was an important job, a good way for a man to earn his bread until he could grow a beard and become a swordsman.

Of course horses were faster than runners over short distances, but not over a long haul. No animal on earth could outrun a trained runner, covering forty or fifty miles a day. When a horse had to stop and graze for hours, a man could slow to a walk for a while and chew on a strip of jerky.

Ivor and Ninian straightened up, put palms against thighs, and watched the royal lips as they recited the message. It was all about details of the coming war, although Ivor was much too busy memorizing the words to understand what they meant. When the litany had ended, it was a moment before he relaxed and thought to breathe.

"Speak it back, Ivor," the king said.

Ivor clenched teeth at the thought that he was being tested again. People were always testing him, as if they couldn't believe he could do a man's job. But perhaps not this time, because speaking back was standard with a long message, and this was a very long and tricky one, all lists and unrelated facts. If the king hadn't asked him to repeat it, Ninian certainly would have done so, as soon as they left the royal presence. He raised his chin and spoke it back to the king.

At the end Constantine looked to Ninian.

"Perfect," Ninian said. "He's got a head like a barrel, sire. Pour in as much as you like, he never gets it wrong. On the way here I asked him to repeat a message he was given eight weeks ago, and he still had it pat, even yet."

"Incredible! I wish I knew how you lads do it. Off you go, then, but do not damage yourselves by trying too hard! An hour or two won't matter, and you're both too valuable to lose."

▶▼◀

With their satchels full of cheese, bannocks, and beef jerky, the runners set off down the hill towards the Tatha River. They hadn't gone far when Ninian said, "You go ahead; I'll follow."

Ivor gave him a suspicious glance. "Why?"

"Because I wasn't lying when I told the king I can't keep up with you. I hold you back. You know the way now, so you go at your pace and I'll go at mine. That's a good safety measure anyway in troubled times. If King Osian of Northumberland has spies around, they would love to capture us, but this way one of us might get through to deliver the king's words and raise the alarm."

Ivor decided that the captain of runners was serious and was giving him orders, so he said, "Aye, sir," and upped his pace. When he looked around, Ninian was half a mile back, and not moving very fast.

▶▼◀

It was late on the following day when Ivor started up the hill to Stiegle Fort. He had been able to run some of the distance by moonlight, for the moon was approaching the full, and he had slept rough, in a haystack. He did not feel nearly as tired as he had done when he arrived at Scone.

Probably that was because he had been able to set his own routine, when to run, when to walk, or rest, instead of being held to Ninian's rhythm. Perhaps some pride of accomplishment helped, too.

The fort was packed with the assembled hirds of the West, well over a thousand men. Ivor headed straight for the mormaor's private quarters, a largish hut alongside the great hall, and even before he reached it, he could hear the party in progress inside it. The guards on the door knew him and admitted him at once; he walked into a noisy carouse where Malcolm was entertaining a score of drunken thanes. Because Ivor brought the king's words, he took precedence over them all, which felt good, a reward for his hard work. Malcolm, who still seemed sober enough, led him off to his own bedroom to hear the message in private.

Of course the first thing he asked was, "Where's Ninian?"

"He sent me on ahead, my lord."

The mormaor smiled. "He warned me he might have to. Let's hear it then."

When Ivor had finished, Malcolm said, "Great heavenly hosts, what a jumble! Say it all again." And after that, "I may need to hear it yet again in the morning. But well done, Ivor of Glenbroch! You give excellent service. Go and rest."

▶▼◀

Runners in the Stiegle fort had their own hut, furnished with four bunks, which was an unusual luxury, much resented by the swordsmen of the hird, who slept on pallets on the floor of the hall. Ninian was married and had his own quarters elsewhere. It was very rare for all six runners to be in Stiegle at the same time, and only then did the most junior of them have to lie on the drafty, smelly floor. That night there was no one else there, so Ivor said his prayers quickly, fell into his favourite bunk, and let the world disappear.

▶▼◀

"Runner!" said a shrill voice in his ear. "Ivor of Glenbroch! *Wake up!*"

Ivor opened one eye and glowered at the diminutive page. "Go to Hell and piss on the Devil."

"Malcolm wants you."

Ivor sat up so fast he almost banged his head on the upper bunk. There was no one else sleeping there. *Not again!* he thought. *Please God, don't let him send me out again so soon!*

But when he marched into the private quarters—which reeked of stale beer and tallow candles—and saw the mormaor's face, he knew that his fears were about to be realized. Give him his due, Malcolm looked as if he had not slept all night. For a moment neither spoke.

"Ninian got here about four hours after you did."

"I never doubted he'd make it, my lord."

"But he's in bad shape. I wouldn't ask you so soon if there wasn't a war on."

It was good to feel important. What use was a job without challenges? "I'm sure you wouldn't, my lord. But there is. Where to?"

"You're sure, now? No blisters?"

"None, my lord. I'm fine."

"Can you go back to the king again?"

Oh, no! "Yes, my lord." Ivor wasn't quite certain that he was lying. His feet and ankles really were still in good shape, and that was what mattered most. So perhaps he would make it all the way.

"I can give you a horse for the first lap. I'll send someone with you to bring it back."

Thinking how hard it would be to get off that horse when the time came, Ivor shook his head. "I can do it, my lord. Speak."

"It'll be four days since you left him, and he was planning to march out yesterday, so you'll not be going to Scone. You'll have to find the army."

Worse! Ivor just nodded.

"Very well, from me to the king, usual titles. Hear my words."

▶▼◀

Technically, the Alban army had already crossed into Lothian, the land wrongly claimed by King Osian of Northumbria, but Ivor was fortunate enough to meet up with a cavalry troop hastening south to join the army. They put him on one of their spare horses and delivered him safely to Constantine's camp, not long after midnight.

He identified himself and demanded that the king be wakened to hear his message. Not many sixteen-year-olds could even dream of doing that, let alone getting away with it, but he was led at once to the royal pavilion. There he had to wait a while, presumably so His Grace could gather his wits and make himself presentable. Then an attendant emerged and told him to go in. The tent was large, with rugs on the floor and made bright by many flickering candles.

"Ivor!" The king was seated on a stool, wearing a woollen robe, but his hair was tousled and the rumpled sheet on his cot showed that he had been asleep. "Great saints, man! Are you mortal?"

"I feel very much so at present, Your Grace."

"I'm sure you do. Then deliver your message. Can you do it sitting down?"

"I don't think so, sire." Ivor came to attention and recited the eight items Malcolm had given him to report. It was a huge relief to be unburdened of all that.

"Well done!" Constantine said. "Very well done. But... how is Malcolm? Did he hesitate or correct himself at all when he was dictating all that?"

That was a breach of the rules! Runners delivered their masters' messages; they were not required to answer questions. Even questions asked by the king? Ivor racked his weary brain and decided that yes, that rule applied even to kings.

"Not that I recall, sire." Which was a lie.

The king smiled faintly. "Now sit. You bring good news and bad news both." He rose and went over to a stout, ironbound chest and lifted the lid. "Repeat that bit about the Lord of the Isles."

Ivor almost panicked. He couldn't remember being told anything, or saying anything, about the Lord of the Isles. Then he recalled Malcolm telling him something about a Northmen-sort-of name, which must be what the king wanted. He fished that item out of his memory like an angler hooking a fish.

"Thus spake Malcolm... 'Ragnvaldr Leifrson has accepted your silver and delivered his younger son, Snorri Ragnvaldson, as hostage for a peaceful summer.' Sire."

"Wonderful!" the king told the contents of the chest. He found what he was looking for and straightened up. "Snorri Ragnvaldson? What a name! Sounds like a bad case of phlegm. We do not kill messengers who bring bad news, but we sometimes reward those who bring very good news, and especially we reward men who perform great feats in our service." Fumbling in a small leather bag, he came to where Ivor had slumped down on a stool. "No, stay where you are. But give me your hand. Mm... I think you'll have to wear it here for a year or two yet."

And he slid a silver ring onto Ivor's thumb—a silver ring engraved with a boar, the king's own symbol.

"Your Grace!" Ivor stared at this treasure in amazement. "I am sworn to Earl Malcolm, sire..."

"Of course you are. I'm not trying to steal you away from his service—but if he ever releases you, I will certainly take you on. That ring merely means that you are a trusted confidant and valued servant of your sovereign. I give them to exceptional people. Now lie down and sleep—right there," the king said, pointing to a rug in the corner. Then he started going around, blowing out candles.

Ivor mumbled thanks and flopped down where he had been directed. Exhausted as he was, he still needed a few minutes to sink into sleep, while he marvelled at the king's gift. His silver buckle meant that he could pass on Malcolm's orders to thanes. But with that ring, he might someday speak with the voice of the king himself.

Chapter 1

"You! Boy! Stop!"

Ivor glanced back in annoyance. He was running—of course. After eight straight days of running back and forth across the country, he ought to be lazing around in Stiegle doing nothing, but the fort was a madhouse, packed with the bored swordsmen of more than two dozen hirds. The town, down by the river, would be in no better shape, so he'd decided to go for a swim in a small loch, which the locals knew but the strangers wouldn't. The water had been bitterly cold, of course, so after his dip he'd decided to take a short run over the moor to dry off. The short run had grown into a longer one, almost as if he could never be happy again unless he was running. Now, when he'd just got the knots worked out and was starting to speed up...

"Boy! Stop!"

Who was he calling a boy? He'd heard the hooves coming behind him for some time and just ignored them, except to increase his speed a little. Now he saw that the speaker was

Swordsman Aodhagán, one of the mormaor's housecarls—big, flabby, and stupid as kelp.

But obviously he was speaking to Ivor, because there was no one else in sight, except a couple of serfs herding sheep in the far distance. Ivor stopped and waited for Fatty to catch up with him. *Saints preserve!* He was riding Patch, so it was no wonder they were coming slowly. Patch was old and not much more than a pony anyway. He should not have to put up with that clumsy greasy lump bouncing on his back. All the best horses had gone south with the army, and all the best men, too, for no ostler worth his oats would have set Patch to carrying fat Aodhagán.

"Malcolm wants you, boy!" Aodhagán roared as he arrived. "Not soon but yesterday!"

Umph! Last night, when Ivor had returned, Malcolm had promised him no more running for at least a week. That didn't mean he might not want to send him somewhere on a horse, though. This was wartime.

"You'd better be lending me your horse, then, swordsman."

The big lunk's face fell. He hadn't thought to bring a spare mount. He looked around in dismay at the empty moorland, and then reluctantly heaved a leg over and slid down. Had he thought about it, he could have pointed out that Ivor could run back to the fort faster than old Patch could. Ivor remembered very little of his mother, but one of her sayings had been that the Lord God must love stupid people, because he made so many of them. All Malcolm's best swordsmen had started south, with only the relics like Aodhagán left behind to guard the chickens and goats. A long walk would do him good.

Ivor lengthened the stirrup leathers as far as they would go and swung aboard Patch, who would find him a much lighter load than Aodhagán. Enjoying the ride, Ivor did not push him hard. The summer sun was already hot enough to bake his back like a bannock, larks were soaring and flowers blooming. Whatever the mormaor's problem, it would have to wait.

He crested the edge of the moor, and started down the cattle track to the Carse of Stiegle. From up there the river looked like a twisted silver ribbon wound along the valley, through fields bright emerald with the first spring growth. A longship was rowing upstream. No others had arrived since Ivor began his run, so unexpected bad news could not explain Malcolm's sudden urgency.

The town was a huddle of shaggy thatch roofs by the water's edge, and the fort a smaller one, set within its rampart on a rise that looked like a molehill from Ivor's viewpoint. The remaining scraps of the army were camped a mile or so upstream, and would leave on the morrow, with the mormaor himself in the lead, and his closest aides around him. Ivor of Glenbroch would be there, and most of the other runners—none of whom wore a silver ring engraved with a boar.

Glenbroch seemed a long way away now.

As he reached the gate of the fort, he caught a closer glimpse of the approaching longship. It looked much like Glenbroch's *Sea Eagle*, which had been Tasgall Mór's ship two months ago. But Tasgall had succeeded Carrak as thane, and might have promoted himself into another vessel. Or it might be another boat from another settlement altogether. The mormaor had summoned his fleet to muster at Abtaraig Bay at a full moon that was only two nights away now. Ivor was secretly hoping he would be sent there, so he would get a chance to meet with his brothers again. He would be surprised if all nine of them weren't present.

"Look what comes!" bellowed one of guards on the gate. "Surely it is the blessed Archangel Micheil himself, bearing holy words from the Lord and riding on a turtle!"

All the horses, wagons, men-at-arms, and just plain people streaming in and out of the fort were making Patch fret nervously. Ivor dismounted and handed his reins to the guard who had spoken.

"Be a good mortal and see my horse back to the stable, please. The mormaor wants me."

"It is the king's man!" shouted another, whose name was Eoghan. "The mormaor needs the help of the king's man!"

So the news of that accursed ring was getting around already? Before Ivor could comment, a horny hand gripped his left arm and then another his right, and he was hoisted bodily.

"Make way! Make way! Make way for the king's man..." Eoghan and another man began running with him, bulling their way through the crowd and bellowing their nonsense. Borne high like a banner, Ivor kicked and shouted, but to no avail—the idiots were showing what they thought of a beardless boy being honoured by the king ahead of all warrior housecarls like themselves.

Worse, he had to go and change before he went to the mormaor, because he was wearing nothing except the very old and skimpy shorts he had worn to go swimming—and would have worn *while* swimming, had there been anyone else at the loch.

The foolery ended abruptly when they ran straight into Malcolm himself, marching along ahead of a retinue of four thanes. Ivor struggled and squealed to his captors to put him down—which they did, but not before the mormaor's brilliant blue eyes began flashing fire. Fortunately Ivor was not the object of his rage.

"Satan's teeth, what do you two think you are doing? That boy is worth ten times more than both of you put together. Eoghan, and whatever your name is—report to the commander for twenty lashes apiece."

"Wait!" Ivor cried. "Please! My lord, I am unhurt. They were only being high spirited. I bear no grudge, my lord."

The mormaor's fury swung around to him, for daring to question his orders, but then he saw the plea in Ivor's eyes, for to have the men punished would merely boost the resentment against Ivor and bring him a lot more harm in future.

"Oh, very well. Since the captain of runners forgives you, I will overlook your offence this time. Get back to your posts!" As the guards fled, he turned to the thanes. "Excuse me, noble lords. Our business will have to wait. Ivor, follow me."

He spun around and marched back the way he had come. Ivor followed as commanded, aware that he had now earned the resentment of four thanes, too.

What had Malcolm called him?

Chapter 2

The guards at the door to the mormaor's private quarters saluted as Malcolm arrived, and one of them opened it for him. It thumped shut as Ivor followed him in. Malcolm turned and renewed his glaring, but he was close enough that he had to glare *up* at Ivor, which wouldn't help his mood. He was a big man, twice as wide as Ivor but a hand shorter. His blue eyes could strike terror into any man; they, and his flaxen hair and beard, told of Northmen ancestors, despite his Pictish name.

"Where the devil have you been, you young fool?"

"I was running on the moor, my lord."

"Running? After eight days of... You're madder than a March hare!"

Before Ivor could reply, or even think of what he could possibly reply, another, quieter, voice spoke up.

"Ivor of Glenbroch!" Malcolm's wife, the Lady Kenina, was a quiet, retiring person, but well loved in Stiegle for her kindness and charity. She was smiling warmly. "Do let me see your ring! It is wonderful that a man so young could have so pleased the king. You honour us all! And I congratulate you, also, on your promotion."

Ivor made a sort of gulping noise. He hadn't misheard!

"Hares may be mad in March," Kenina said, "but they run very fast the other eleven months. Perhaps not as fast as you, though?"

"I... I've never tried to catch one, my lady."

Kenina laughed. "Wait until this foolish war is over before you try. Now stop growling, Malcolm, and tell him why you summoned him, and why you value his service so highly."

Malcolm snarled only, "Come with me." He strode off in a swirl of his fine linen gown, on feet clad in fur.

He unlocked an unobtrusive door that Ivor had never noticed before, and locked it as soon as Ivor followed him in. The little room was stuffy, smelly, and dim, with a single parchment-covered window. It held half a dozen solid chests and a large table, so that there was barely room to move.

"Ninian's gone."

"No! What—"

"I don't mean he's dead!" Malcolm said. "I promoted him to quartermaster and sent him off to organize the army commissariat before those thieves down there in Northumbria ruin me. He's too old to be a runner anyway. I asked who should replace him and he had the insolence to tell me that if I promoted anyone but you, I was a brick-headed idiot. He said that he'd never seen anyone run as well as you and have a memory to match."

Ivor smiled disbelievingly. However untrue, the compliments felt good. He did not say so, because Malcolm had not finished yet. "Your father, your brother Angus, and your other brothers—all great men. You're sprung from fine stock, lad, and I've been very impressed by you over the last... what? Two months?"

"Nine weeks, my lord." All this flattery was very nice, but no one would ever take Ivor seriously until his face could grow hair that was visible at more than arm's length.

"And you certainly impressed His Grace." Malcolm pointed at the thumb that wore the boar ring. "But despite the king and despite Ninian, I'd already decided to appoint you captain of runners. You'll get double your present pay and a room of your own. Meanwhile I have another mission for you—look at this."

He turned to the long table. Now that his eyes had adjusted to the gloom, Ivor saw that the boards were painted blue, but most of the surface was covered with piles of green plaster. *Two groats a week?* He would be rich!

"I beg your pardon, my lord?"

"I said you're shivering. Stupid of me. I'll get a blanket for you."

"I'm fine, my lord. I'm shivering with excitement, is all."

"Sure? I don't want you to catch a chill. You play chess?"

"A little." There were four men in Glenbroch that Ivor had never managed to beat even once, but one of them was his brother Jock, who was glen champion, so he didn't count.

Malcolm was holding a finely carved wooden box. He took out a white castle and placed it on the green plaster, near the centre.

"Then remember that this is roughly where Scone is, the king's seat. You are looking at an angel's view of Alba, but you're a very short-sighted angel, because this doesn't show any details. My side is east, toward Jerusalem, and this coast is Alba, from the Firth of Forth in the south, here, all the way north, up to Moray and Caithness."

Ivor had heard of those. Their mormaors had not always been as loyal to the king as Malcolm was.

"White king," Malcolm said, producing it. "Constantine must be somewhere about here by now, leading his army south to meet... This black castle can be Bjorn, who styles himself lord of Lothian, but is just a hunting dog of King Osian and will shortly be chased back south to York, where he belongs. Somewhere beyond that, over by the door if the table were big enough, would be Mercia and Wessex, the realms of the Saxons. You with me so far?"

"Yes, my lord."

"On your side is the west coast. Ireland's behind you. This will be Stiegle." He leaned across to place the second white castle in front of Ivor. "And a white knight for my army beside it."

Then he produced a second black castle and put it in the south to represent King Osian of Northumbria. And a second white knight, to be placed in the far northwest, the home of the Northmen and the Lord of the Isles.

And finally a white pawn. "Catch! That's you."

Ivor set the white pawn beside the Stiegle castle and the Malcolm knight.

Malcolm put the box away. "That's the present state of play. All right?"

"Yes, my lord." It was scary to be even a lowly pawn in a game of kings and armies.

"Now in this game, King Constantine is allowed to move two pieces at once, so he takes his own army south, against Bjorn, and sends me south to distract Osian, because we don't want that scoundrel coming to the aid of his puppet." Malcolm moved the white king south; Ivor moved the white knight to match. "We'll teach Osian a lesson and pick up some loot to cover expenses. How do you like this position, chess player?"

Ivor took his time, studying the map and remembering winter tales told in the hall in Glenbroch. He thought Jock, brother number five, would say that his ass felt cold. "Ireland, my lord?"

"Ireland's behind you, but the little princes there are all fighting one another, so they won't bother us. Anything else?

Ivor's gaze wandered north. The Stiegle castle looked rather vulnerable, guarded by a single pawn, him. Of course Scone was left naked also, but Constantine ruled all the east coast, to the farthest north. North of the Malcolm's earldom lay the islands and rugged shores of the Northmen. Somewhere in there was Dunfaol, the Lord of the Isles' lair. While Malcolm and his hird of swordsmen were away, what was to stop Ragnvaldr sending his fleet south to ravage Stiegle? Or Glenbroch? Or many other undefended places?

So it was Ivor's move? "The Lord of the Isles, my lord? How sure are you that he's a white piece?"

Malcolm nodded grimly. "Well done, laddie! Aye, in this game pieces can change colour. The Irish are fighting amongst themselves like cats in a sack, but the Northmen are dangerous. Earl Ragnvaldr Leifrson, the Lord of the Isles, has promised to leave us alone this summer and just send his young hotheads to have some sport with the Irish. I bought him off with enough silver to choke him, and he's sent me his younger son to be hostage for his good faith."

That was Snorri Ragnvaldson, whom the king had called a bad case of phlegm. Surely even a barbaric Northman would not betray his own son? But Ivor turned again to meet the icy blue eyes, and his shivering returned. The mormaor was waiting for him, so after a moment he took up the white Ivor pawn and moved it north to join that questionable white knight. He would be going by sea, not on his hard-worked feet this time. He looked up expectantly.

"Well done!" the mormaor said again. "I now have reason

DAVE DUNCAN

to believe that Ragnvaldr may not be as secure on his throne as we would all like."

Not surprising! When the Northmen weren't fighting their neighbours, they beat up their friends. If Earl Ragnvaldr's thanes caught him burying Malcolm's silver under his bed instead of sharing it out, they would make him the previous Lord of the Isles very speedily. Was it even possible that Ragnvaldr Leifrson suspected a plot against him and had sent his son Snorri south, officially as a hostage, but really for his own safety?

If the Lord of the Isles had changed sides, Ivor's mission looked anything but routine. "Any word on the challengers, my lord?"

"Nothing definite. A man called Thorfinn Fleinn was causing trouble last summer—Thorfinn the Spear. From what I've heard, he's more than half pagan, a devilish throwback to his ancestors. The Northmen's faith in our Saviour isn't always as firm as it should be."

That was true in the wilder parts of Alba, too. Ivor's sometime friend Rorie of Ytter wore a Thor's hammer instead of a cross when he was alone.

Ivor dragged his mind back to the practical problem. If the Northmen did not stay bought, King Constantine's strategy would collapse into a pile of ashes, with all of western Alba left without defences and a raving bloodthirsty pagan pirate poised to attack. So what did Malcolm expect a sixteen-year-old with a good memory and long legs to do about it? Everyone else had been sent south. *This was far more than a runner's job, even a captain of runners'!* Suddenly Ivor was scared enough to stare right back at those deadly sky-blue eyes and wait until His Lordship spoke.

"That chest by your feet, lad?"

Ivor looked down. He had barely noticed it earlier, except to be careful not to stub a toe on it. It was old and its carved panels had split in places. It had no hinges, just a lid that fitted over the top, held by three loops of rope, two crosswise and one lengthwise. Their knots were sealed with wax bearing the mormaor's seal.

"It's full of silver," Malcolm said. "*Sea Eagle*'s on its way. It's as fast as any ship in the fleet."

"I saw it in the river as I was coming up the hill, my lord."

"And your brother is master now. I've sent down word that he's to keep his crew aboard and be ready to leave as soon as my runner arrives. That's you. I want you to go north and sort out this mess for me."

Oh, Queen of Heaven! But that had been obvious for several minutes. Ivor straightened up, laid his hands against his thighs, and fixed his gaze on the mormaor's lips, waiting for the words.

Malcolm shook his head. "I can't give you a straight message, because I don't know what situation you'll find there. Remember that Ragnvaldr Leifrson likes to call himself *King* of the Isles. If his head's still on his shoulders, he will expect to be given royal honours. You can do that personally—Ivor of Glenbroch can bow and scrape as much as he expects—but when you quote me, remember that I greet the scoundrel as 'Earl Ragnvaldr, *Lord* of the Isles, and dearly loved brother in Christ'. You must NOT quote me as calling him a king! Give him a bag of silver and wish him luck in Ireland. Assure him that his son arrived safely and is well..."

Malcolm frowned. "He's sure to suspect a double-cross, so be wary. He'll wonder if we're up to what we're afraid he's up to—that you've been sent to spy on him, so that as soon as *his* hird is out of the way, *we* can attack *his* lands. In that case he may 'invite' you and your crew to join in the Irish caper. You'll have to accept. Try not to get killed.

"But, if Thorfinn or someone like him is raising trouble, give Ragnvaldr the whole box of silver, and he'll put it to good use, understand?"

Ivor nodded. There still had to be more.

Yes...

"But," the mormaor said with a sigh, "if you find someone else is top dog now, then you'll have to use your best judgment and try to get out alive. Give him the silver, the humblest titles you think you can get away with, my best wishes on his succession, and some glib talk about the long friendship between the Western Isles and Alba."

"And promise him a share of the Northumbrian loot, my lord?"

"Might as well. He'll certainly demand more than you offer. Mostly you'll have to make it up as you go along. That's why I'm sending you—because you know my style by now."

And because there was no one else left in Stiegle to send? Or because he was expendable? Ivor nodded, his mouth very dry.

"Or you may find there's a civil war going on there. In which case... do try not to get killed! Throw the silver on the floor and let them kill one another off fighting over it." Malcolm smiled thinly. "I am joking there, but you might be able to sway a lot of votes with that chest.

"And finally, Captain of Runners, if you run into the Northmen's fleet heading this way, no matter who's in charge of it, you turn around and boil the sea all the way back here to warn us, understand? Clear?"

"Aye, my lord." This all sounded like a death sentence.

"Don't sell yourself short," the mormaor said quietly. "You can do it. That first day I met you, Ivor, you impressed me greatly. Not just because you ran up the hill faster than Ninian. You have ten years on him, so that wasn't very surprising. But when I tried ragging you in the hall, you stood up to me, and no one's done that in ages. I bullied harder, and you glared furiously and still didn't crumble. In a lad of your years that took true nerve!"

And that really was flattering! "I have nine older brothers, my lord."

Malcolm smiled the smile of a man who has too many troubles to smile. "Then that explains it! On this mission, consult Angus if you must, but keep him in the dark as long as you can, and certainly don't tell his crew how tangled the strings are in this—you do not want to start a mutiny! You are to make the decisions, not Angus, understand? Now, a message to your brother. Ready?"

"Yes, my lord." Hands against thighs, watch his lips...

"Hear my words. My usual titles... *to Angus, tanist of Glenbroch, master of* Sea Eagle, *and his crew, greetings! You are hereby required to convey the bearer of this message to such place or places as he wishes, and provide him with all necessary assistance in the performance of the duties we have laid upon him.* Speak it back to me."

Ivor's training held, and he spoke the awful words without a stumble. Malcolm listened intently, and then nodded. He tossed Ivor a leather pouch that clinked. "In case you can get away with a smaller bribe. Get your gear and go. I'll see the silver is waiting for you at the gate."

Ivor bowed and turned away.

"Ivor!"

"My lord?"

For the first time ever, Ivor thought he saw Malcolm uncertain. "Ragnvaldson is married, but *if* you have to deal with someone else... and *if* the subject arises... you are *not* to bring it up on your own, understand? But *if* the new Lord of the Isles should ask about my daughter, you will *not* mention that she is already betrothed! If necessary deny it, and accept any messages on the subject that he wishes to send to me, understand?"

Ivor nodded unhappily. Telling a runner to lie seemed very wrong. "Yes, my lord." There was evidently worse to come.

The mormaor was looking even more uneasy than before, biting his lip and not meeting Ivor's eye. After a moment he said quietly, "You wear the king's ring. When Constantine sends a message to Ragnvaldr, he addresses him as, *Earl Ragnvaldr, Lord of the Isles, our loyal and beloved mormaor.*"

Ivor felt the hair on his scalp try to rise. "You are saying that I can put words in the *king's* mouth, my lord?"

Still the mormaor did not look him in the eye. "If I am ever asked, I will deny saying so, understand? But desperate problems can require desperate solutions. Do whatever you must to keep the Northmen's knives off our throats this summer. God and his angels go with you, lad."

Chapter 3

Still trying to understand the tangled web of instructions he'd been given—very unlike Malcolm's usual short, clear orders—Ivor left the little room and headed for the main door.

"Captain of Runners!"

He turned. Lady Kenina had gone, and the angel standing by the fireplace was her daughter, Meg, who was certainly the most gorgeous creature the Good Lord had created since Eve. Ivor dreamed of her, and suspected that every man in the fort did too. She was three months younger than he, and had she been any other man's daughter—and not already betrothed, of course—Ivor of Glenbroch would be sleeping on her doorstep and spending everything he had to buy her gifts. She had never spoken to him before, but he had noticed her looking at him several times. Eagerly he strode across to her. She wore a sky blue gown, exactly the colour of her eyes, and her long flaxen hair was unbound to indicate that she was unmarried.

He bowed. "My lady?" His heart was thumping. He wasn't decently dressed, washed, or combed to be seen by a lady. *She had spoken to him! She had spoken to him!* He should not have come so close, because she had to look up to him. She was dainty—perfection had no need of size to impress, no need to shout. But her eyes weren't even level with his collar bones; she had a good view of his bony and very hairless chest. He couldn't back away now without drawing attention to his mistake.

"I just want to congratulate you on your promotion."

"You are very kind, my lady."

"My father speaks very highly of you, Captain."

Gulp. *Tongue-tied moron! What did he say now? Lovely weather?* "Um, thank you, my lady." He could feel his face starting to turn scarlet.

She must be accustomed to men melting into sheep when she spoke to them. She smiled. God's nails, she was gorgeous! "Is that not the thane of Glenbroch's ship coming up the river?"

"No, my lady—I mean yes, my lady. I mean yes, that is *Sea Eagle*, which was Tanist Tasgall's ship, but it is by custom the tanist's, and your honoured father tells me that the master is the current tanist, my Brother Angus, because former Tanist Tasgall succeeded to the thaneship..." Oh, sweet Heaven, he was babbling! She must know all that, because she was Tasgall's betrothed, or would be as soon as the summer's campaign was over.

So that was the real reason Lady Meg had bothered to tell him what her father thought of him: so she could ask about her fiancé. Chief Stammerer Ivor of Glenbroch must be as a red as a summer sunset now. He could feel a trickle of sweat running down beside his ribs.

"May I see the ring the king gave you?" She took his hand to look at it. Her fingers were warm and gentle. "We are all very proud of you."

Gulp. "Thank you, my lady."

The lady smiled. "Meg?"

Gasp. "Meg."

"My father is very worried about the Northmen. Do come back safe, Ivor."

Embarrassed beyond words, he just nodded and turned away—and was horrified to see her father standing outside the door to the table room, staring coldly at this upstart, half-naked youth who had the impudence to gab with his daughter when he should be attending to his duties. Ivor shot across the room in a rush and was gone, out into the fresh air, cool on his heated face.

Gibbering coward! But more than one thing about that little conversation had been odd. When Ivor had told Lady Meg that her fiancé was not sailing up the river and about to come calling, surely she should have been disappointed? But what he'd thought he had seen appear for a brief moment on those angelic features had been relief.

When he reached the runners' shed, only Edan was there, sitting on a three-legged stool by the door and idly polishing his belt buckle. He looked up with interest as Ivor began dragging everything out of his pack to reach the ragged old clothes he had worn back home in Glenbroch.

"Good one?" he asked, knowing he would hear no details of Ivor's mission.

"Get to sit down all the way."

The older man thought he meant horseback and made a joke about calluses. Edan's memory was flawless, but he was not noted for the speed of his wits, which must be why Ivor was being sent to the northern chopping block, not he.

"You hear that Ninian's been promoted?"

"Yes," Ivor said.

"Who d'yu think'll be our new captain? Ilgarach?"

Ivor didn't want to tell him. Why? Other men bragged about promotion and honours. He really must be as crazy as the March hare Malcolm had called him.

"That's up to the mormaor to decide."

He dressed hurriedly, stuffed his good clothes in his pack, and slung his cloak on his shoulders—the cloak his mother had woven for him just before she died. It had been years before he had been tall enough to wear it. He ran out the door, shouting thanks for Edan's, "God go with you, kid."

Before leaving the fort, he ran around to the chapel. So many men were departing for the war now that Father Crinan was working from dawn to dusk, hearing confessions and shriving. About a dozen swordsmen were sitting around on the grass outside, bragging about the thrashing they were going to inflict on the Northumbrian dwarfs. That probably kept their own spirits up and did no harm to their foes, at least not yet. When the current penitent emerged, they waved Ivor forward, knowing that his business must be more urgent than theirs.

As he walked into the cool dimness of the little church, he tried to recall exactly what sins he had managed to find time for in the last few weeks. Then remembered all Malcolm's flattery and the king's ring and his promotion. So he confessed to pride, mostly. It was God who deserved the credit for strong legs and a good memory.

Pride went before a fall.

When the state of his soul had been attended to, he headed for the gate. As Malcolm had promised, the chest of silver was waiting there, stoutly bound to two poles, and four brawny serfs stood alongside. A horse he did not know was already saddled for him, and four mounted housecarls were waiting to escort him down the hill. They did not salute him.

"Ready?" their leader said, his tone implying, *Ready at last?*

"Ready. Don't go too fast for the porters."

The serfs glumly gripped the ends of the poles and hoisted their burden shoulder high. Obviously it was not a burden to be taken lightly. Ivor swung up onto his horse's broad back.

"Um, Captain of Runners?" asked a very humble voice. Ivor looked down and saw Eoghan and his fellow troublemaker. "Captain, we just wanted to say thank you for keeping us off the whipping post."

For a moment Ivor was completely at a loss for words—he'd never had housecarls apologize to him before. "That's all right," he said. "Do me a favour?"

"Yes, sir!" they chorused. "Anything!"

"Kill some of the Northumbrian scum for me!"

With their promises ringing in his ears, Ivor rode off with his escort. Well, that had gone rather well. He felt almost better about winning two armed thugs' approval than he did about his promotion to chief runner. It was weird. He knew where he was with such men, but not with highborn ladies.

None of the housecarls were much older than he, so they were much displeased at having to escort a mere boy, silver buckle or not. They did not seem to realize that a chest so heavy must contain more than clothes or documents. It clinked, and once Ivor thought he saw a gleam of silver through one of the cracks in the panels. Nor did his guards know that he was brother to a quarter of *Sea Eagle*'s crew, so when they reached the spot where *Sea Eagle* was moored, they were surprised to be loudly cheered.

Built for war, the ship seemed sinister compared to the chubby little fishing boats alongside it. More than fifty feet long, about eight wide, it was slender and fast. Drawing only two feet of water, it could travel far upstream on rivers, or run up on a beach, and instantly spill out its crew armed with swords, axes, and shields. The men leaped ashore now, but unarmed and laughing, led by four other sons of Bracken—Tomas, Jock, Fergus, and Lachlan, all roaring out insults:

"The runaway's been captured!"

"The lost sheep's found!"

"Must be a spare oar; it's too thin to be a mast."

The rest, Glenbroch men all, followed and joined in the abuse, but were careful not to become so offensive that the family might close ranks around its new hero. The housecarls looked on disdainfully. Villagers, fishermen, and sailors from other boats watched with amusement.

Big Angus came last, and his arrival calmed the friendly riot. Shouts went up for a judgement. For the second time that morning Ivor was hoisted bodily—this time so that his riding shoes could be removed, then he was set down barefoot on the mud. Angus was already shoeless, as was traditional on ships. They stood nose-to-nose

"Aye!" the rest of the family roared in unison, indicating that Ivor had at last outgrown the eldest, and so was now tallest of the ten brothers. Ivor had his doubts about that verdict, but he and Angus grinned and embraced. More hugging and back-slapping followed.

A sudden pain in his throat reminded him that he was very likely leading them all to their deaths. He broke free and addressed the contemptuous housecarls. "I thank you, swordsmen. Master, will you have that box stowed aboard, please?"

He pointed, which was a mistake, because sunlight flashed off his ring. No one commented, but he wished he had thought to remove it and hide it in his pack.

Jock and Fergus went to lift the chest and discovered its

THE RUNNER AND THE SAINT

weight. They shot startled looks at him. It took four men to lift it aboard, a job that needed care, for it would spring the planks of the hull if they dropped it. Gratings had to be lifted and ballast removed to make a place for it and it was some time before Angus was satisfied with the ship's trim and the gratings could be replaced.

"You bring orders for me, Runner?" Angus said, and there was a sudden hush.

Ivor glanced meaningfully at the crowd that had gathered around to watch. His message was to the whole crew, but the onlookers had no right to hear what he had to say. "Later, if you please, Tanist. Can you still catch the tide?"

"We can try. *All aboard!*"

The rowers scampered to their places and took up their oars. Ivor went to the stern, knowing he would sit beside the helmsman. He might beg a brief turn at rowing later, but his arms could never keep up with the older men's. Legs, now, were a different matter. There he could hold his own against anyone.

Pride, again.

In moments oars were flashing through silver water. Under Angus's expert direction, *Sea Eagle* slid out of the melee of smaller boats, spun in her own length, and set off downstream, powered by forty brawny arms. For Ivor, it was wonderful to be back among the smells and sounds of a ship, and especially this one: the one that had brought him to Stiegle on the fateful day when he had first met Malcolm and been appointed a runner, an honour he had not appreciated at the time. He sat beside the helmsman and watched the grinning—and soon sweating—faces of the rowers. Each one sat on his sea chest, sliding back and forth on a leather cushion as he rowed. They had brought no water boy, so that would be Ivor's job again. Meanwhile he could enjoy the familiar surge as each sweep of the oars bit; the creaking of ropes and oarlocks, the thump of the helmsman's beat.

What Angus didn't know about managing people wasn't known to anyone else either, so he had put himself three rows forward among the rowers and set Lachlan to take the steering oar, so now the crew could not suspect their captain of worming secrets out of the passenger without sharing them. Lachlan, brother number nine, was a notorious gossip and chattered incessantly, telling news of who had been born, married, or buried in Glenbroch over the last nine weeks.

Ivor tried to appear attentive as the peaceful river banks flowed by, but his mind kept chewing on the dangers ahead. It was strange that Malcolm had not told him how he had heard the news of Ragnvaldr Leifrson's downfall. Was the story reliable or just a rumour? Even the king had been happy to hear of the hostage, Snorri, but what if Snorri had brought news of rebellion festering again in the north? Mormaor Malcolm's careful plans might turn into historic disaster.

He felt even sorrier that the mormaor had no senior men left to help him with the problem. The correct response to such news should be a state embassy—a couple of grey-bearded thanes and a bishop or two—sent to negotiate a new treaty. Not a peach-faced kid. The Northmen would cut his throat and keep the silver.

Malcolm had named three possible outcomes for Ivor's mission, and every one of them was fraught with disaster. If he met the Northmen's fleet heading south to Alba, he was supposed to outrun it and bring a warning home, but *Sea Eagle* carried only twenty rowers, while some of the Northmen's ships would be twice as long, with crews of forty or more, and thus much faster. Besides, how could one ship warn the entire coast in time to do any good? The raiders could pick their targets, and Malcolm's forces would be far away in Northumbria.

Even if Earl Ragnvaldr were still top dog in the Isles, he would be suspicious to find *Sea Eagle* skulking in his waters. As Malcolm had said, he would suspect a double-cross, suspecting that Alba was waiting to attack his coast as soon as he sent his own fleet off to Ireland. At best he would impound *Sea Eagle* and clap the crew in chains. If he did take them along with him to Ireland, he would put them in the front line to be killed first.

And what if Ragnvaldr had been deposed by the ominously-named Thorfinn Fleinn or some other rebel? Certainly the new earl would be breathing fire to rally his supporters, and Alba was the closest target.

There seemed to be no way to come out of this mission alive.

"Um... what?"

"I said you don't look like a happy runner, Runt," Lachlan said.

"I was daydreaming."

"Looked more like nightmaring to me. Want to share?"

Ivor glanced at the landscape. Sedge and sand dunes showed that they were almost at the coast, and the river still ran strongly, so the tide was not turning yet. More important, if he got thrown overboard here, he could swim ashore! "Good idea. Heave to."

Lachlan beat a signal to the crew to back water and *Sea Eagle* slowed to the river's pace. Ivor exchanged nods with Angus, and they both stood up. Ivor put his palms against his thighs and spoke the hateful words, although they burned his throat.

"Malcolm of Stiegle, Mormaor of the West, prince of Alba, admiral of the fleet, member of the king's council, lord of high justice, Thane of Invervuic, Thane of Bragoran, Thane of Ardenfort, et cetera, sends greetings to his stalwart servant, Angus, tanist of Glenbroch, master of Sea Eagle, *and his crew, saying: You are hereby required to convey the bearer of this message to such place or places as he wishes, and provide him with all necessary assistance in*

the performance of the duties we have laid upon him. Thus spake Mormaor Malcolm."

Ivor watched the smiles turn to frowns as the men worked it out: this slip of a boy had been set in command over them? He would be giving the orders? That must be why Malcolm had chosen Ivor and this ship, for setting any other runner in command of any other crew, might well create a mutiny. They would head straight back to Stiegle for confirmation of such an outrageous situation.

Only Angus took the news without a hint of offence. He called for a cheer for the mormaor, and got a thin one. Then, "Where to, Runner?"

"North, if you please, Tanist, to the Western Isles."

The crew booed, to show that they all wanted to go south, to the war, so that they could kill enemies and thus show that they were real men. Angus came aft to be steersman again, and soon *Sea Eagle* was once more speeding onward to her fate.

"Who gave you that ring?" Angus murmured into his beard.

Men were expected to boast of such honours. Ivor held out his right thumb and tapped a fingernail on the boar. "Him."

"And what's inside that box that's spoiling the draft of my ship?"

"Bullion."

"God's wounds, Ivor me-lad, but I'm proud of my baby brother! No other Glenbroch man has ever risen so high so fast!"

The higher they go, the farther they fall.

"I've always been proud of you, Angus. And all the others." Ivor bit his lip hard and turned away to study the surf breaking over the bar.

"Well, you don't need to look up to me any more, Little Brother. *We're* all bragging about being related to *you*."

Ivor wanted to scream; he wasn't ready for this yet! He was certain to foul everything up, and then where would their hero be? Dead, of course. Angus stopped talking while he skillfully guided *Sea Eagle* through the channel. Soon he called on the men to raise the sail. Wafted by a southeasterly breeze, they headed out over a calm sea.

The hills of the mainland began to fade into a summer haze, and the men had time on their hands, time to interrogate their passenger. They came at him in groups, usually letting one of his brothers lead the questioning. Lachlan of Bracken, who was two years older than Ivor, was probably the youngest of the sailors. None of the others had been among his childhood friends; a few had been his friends' older brothers, and the rest were friends' fathers or uncles. They all wanted to hear of his adventures, and he shared as much as he could. The unmarried ones wanted to hear about the girls in Stiegle, for Glenbroch was currently suffering from a shortage of those desirable properties. They refused to believe Ivor's excuse that he hadn't had time to get to know any of them, which was almost true.

News that Ivor wore the king's ring had flashed around the ship. Everyone wanted to see it and regard it with awe: no Glenbroch man had ever met a king before, let alone been so honoured by one. The one question Ivor could not answer, because he honestly did not know, was why he had been so rewarded. So far as he could see, he had done nothing more than his duty.

When he said so to Angus, Angus smiled and said, "Was it difficult?"

"Sometimes. Why?"

"Then that would be it."

Which didn't make much sense. Surely every man was expected to do his duty whether it was difficult or not?

It was good to hear the news, to see familiar faces, and listen to the familiar lilt of Glenbroch tongues. For two months Ivor had suffered pangs of homesickness whenever he had found the time, but now he sensed that an unexpected hedge had grown up between the cub and the den. The glen had not changed, but he had. He was no longer just the stringy kid with a slick pair of heels. Ever since he had ridden off to find that wizard, Rorie of Ytter, he had been cloaked in an aura of the uncanny, and his latest astonishing rise confirmed it.

Of course they all wanted to know where *Sea Eagle* was bound, and why, but Ivor obeyed the mormaor's orders and refused to tell them even as much as he had revealed to Angus. Fergus, brother number seven, was especially persistent, which was typical of him.

"How're we ever going to live this down?" he griped. "Every red-blooded Alban is heading south and you're taking us north. You're dragging us away from all the fighting."

Ivor said, "Just pray that you're right, Brother. If we have to fight here, we have no army to help us." That shut him up.

Soon after noon, land came into sight ahead. In an hour or two it resolved into a line of hilly islands, and Angus ordered the men back to the oars, because wind could eddy around hills, and he did not trust *Sea Eagle*'s maneuverability under sail. Scanning the scenery as it went by, some of it quite close, Ivor saw no signs of inhabitants, just a few roofless ruins—lonely outposts raided ages ago by the Northmen, their inhabitants slain out of hand or carried off into slavery. Many of the crew could be heard muttering prayers for the souls of the dead.

Later, as the sun drew near to setting, Angus took another tour with the steering oar and beckoned his passenger to come aft for a conference.

"Your mission, is it urgent?"

Ivor said, "Yes."

"The moon's close to the full. We can sail through the night if you want."

That was unusual—because of the obvious dangers, because navigators needed landmarks and usually stayed close to shore, and because hard work made rowers use up their food and water at an astonishing rate. But *Sea Eagle*'s crew had enjoyed an easy day, so Angus could conserve the rations, and the weather was too good to waste; in fact the crew were talking of it being a good portent, a sign that the Lord approved of their young wizard's mission.

The tanist's offer was also a hint that it was time for Ivor to reveal where they were going.

"I have to find the Lord of the Isles."

"Glad to hear it." The big man's beard parted in a grin of white teeth.

"Why?"

"Because anyone taking a chest as weighty as that one to anyone else in the Western Isles would be up to no good."

"I'm supposed to make sure that *he* isn't up to no good."

This time Angus laughed. "You'll have your work cut out for you, Runt! Sorry, Runner. Mustn't call you that any more."

"Does my heart good to hear it. Can I call you 'Little Brother' now? Will he be at Dunfaol?"

"He could be anywhere, I'm thinking. Talk wi' Jock. He knows the Isles better than most of us. Go and tell him to come and take the helm."

Jock was known among the brothers as the Fox, the chess champion, the one credited with the best wits. He was slighter than the others, but had the same dark hair and complexion. It was typical of his quickness that he had barely settled the steering oar in the crook of his elbow and

Angus had just left, when he said, "So what do you want to ask me, Runner?"

"Please don't call me that!"

"Runt?"

"Much better. I need to find the Lord of the Isles, so I need to find someone who knows where he is at the moment. Is there a town I can ask at?"

"There's no towns at all in his domain, Runt. It's all mountains and glens, mainland and islands both. Your best bet from here would be Eyin Helga. You know it?"

"The Holy Island?"

"Aye. Go on. What else did Father Sweeney manage to stuff into your pagan little head?"

Ivor thought for a moment, and then recited in his best imitation of the ancient priest's creaky voice: " 'It's a very small island, but the monastery there was founded by the holy Saint Callum, who came from Ireland and went on to convert all Alba to the True Faith. It became one of the holiest places in Christendom. The kings of Dalriada were crowned there and buried there. The evil Northmen under Ingvarr the Tusk sacked it a hundred years ago....' Then the old bore went on to tell us all about his pilgrimage there. Several times."

Jock snorted. "I'd forgotten that memory of yours."

"Dougal trained me."

"Dougal used to take bets on how many speeches he could cram into your head at the same time without your mixing them up. He never lost, that I recall. But, aye, there's still a few monks live on Eyin Helga, and people do still go there on pilgrimage. I'm saying that the monks may have a fair idea of what's afoot in the Isles. That's if you can get them to admit it, worldly affairs not being sacred enough for their taste. Aye, let's head there first. A few prayers won't hurt any of us."

He checked the wake, then said, "After that, you'll have to make your own decisions."

Chapter 4

Night sailing was so rare that Ivor was not the only one who had never slept aboard a moving ship before, and he found it a strange process, none too pleasant. The crew had fed on smoked fish, dried apples, and oatcakes; as *Sea Eagle* rode the swell, he began to think that he had feasted too heartily. Two men kept watch at all times, and there was little room between the lockers for everyone to stretch out on the gratings. He seemed to waken every few minutes as smelly feet were pushed in his face.

And the moon was very bright.

Morning found them too far from land to be comfortable. With a single square sail, they could do little but run before the wind; only oars would take them on any other course. Angus steered her as close to easterly as he could, and soon a couple of peaks came into view. After a heated discussion, the men who had been this way before agreed that they were on course for the holy island and making good time, too. They should arrive soon after dawn tomorrow.

The weather remained kind and by evening they knew they were close. But were they close enough? They were arriving from the south, where there was a good beach, but to run onto a lee shore in the dark was courting disaster. Should they press on or heave to and wait for dawn? Angus called for a vote. For a few moments no one spoke, because to do so would be to risk seeming either cowardly or foolhardy. Then Fergus yelled, "Let the king's man decide."

Others agreed: "Aye! What does the kid want?"

Two months ago, Ivor would have sensed that his courage was being tested and jumped right into the trap, but he had learned a lot in Stiegle.

He said, "I'm not master of this ship, just a passenger. Brother?"

Big white teeth showed in the tanist's beard as he smiled. "Hands up to go on?"

Every hand rose—some quickly, others following more cautiously, but no one was going to risk being a shirker. So they went on, for a second night at sea.

A few minutes later, Ivor was shocked to realize that Angus had arranged that little confab to give him exactly what he wanted—the crew's agreement to risk their own necks. He was even more shocked to see that nobody else aboard seemed to have worked that out.

▶▼◀

As the summer sun set, rowers dozed at their stations, ready to jump into action. Ivor stretched out on the gratings and tried to sleep. He must have succeeded, because he came awake with a jolt when a cry from the lookout in the bow announced land ahead. Moonlight shone on breakers not a stone's throw away, and surf boomed.

With every man on his feet and Angus bellowing orders, the sail was lowered, oars run out. For a moment the wind and current seemed to be winning, pushing their prey into the teeth of destruction, but *Sea Eagle*'s symmetrical shape let it reverse course without turning. With the rowers facing the bow, the ship fought free of the eddies and backed away from the reef.

Unable to contribute anything, Ivor stood amidship, holding tight to the mast, disgusted that the narrow escape had left him trembling like a frightened child. A ferocious argument had begun around the two crewman who had been lookouts and were now trying to shift the blame onto a wisp of cloud that had covered the moon for a brief minute. Any less brief, and Runner Ivor's career would have come to a very nasty end. Drowning was a fearful death, but being battered to pulp on jagged rocks must be worse.

As soon as Angus judged that the ship was out of danger, he called a halt and led the crew in a brief prayer of thanksgiving for their deliverance. When all the amens had been said, another argument broke out, led by Jock of Bracken, who was pointing at the skyline and insisting that this was Eyin Helga itself, Saint Callum's holy island, their destination, Heavenly Father be praised!

Others objected that it was barely midnight, according to the moon, and they couldn't possibly have arrived yet. But gradually the rest of the experts came around and agreed that the little hill did look like Eyin Helga, and the best landing beach ought to be straight ahead. The rocks that had so nearly killed them were the tip of a headland, and now *Sea Eagle* was facing a sheltered bay. Whether this was their destination or not, the decision then was easy.

"We're going in," Angus bellowed. "Runner, take bow watch."

Ivor hurried forward. Last summer, when he had been water boy on *Petrel*, Angus had taught him the rudiments of a bow watch's duties, but he had never performed them without an older man beside him, and certainly never by moonlight. He took up a spare oar and lowered it into the sea until he judged its end was about three feet below the keel. His task was to warn the helmsman when he felt bottom. There were nasty stories of men on bow watch giving that notice by being catapulted overboard.

Moonlight gleamed on the surf as it rolled up the beach. Running too hard into a steep beach could damage the hull. The trick was to judge the height of the swell just before it broke, because that told you the depth of water at that point. Angus could judge that much better than he could, but Angus was farther away, and the light was poor. Once the waves began to break and topple into foam they would carry the ship forward, instead of just rocking it up and down.

Thump... thump... went the helmsman's beat, signalling the stroke. Ivor struggled to watch the breakers while holding the heavy oar steady and upright. But soon his attention wandered to the land beyond, because there were lights coming down the dark hill toward the beach, three of them. *Lights?* Who would come to a beach in the middle of a brief summer night? He thought of wreckers, human vultures waiting to gather up the loot when a ship was smashed to flotsam. They would knife any sailor lucky enough to come ashore alive, but no one had known that *Sea Eagle* was coming, and there hadn't been time for a watcher to give an alarm. He considered shouting a warning to Angus, but that might distract him from his work of bringing in the ship.

The bow dipped, the oar lurched and almost dragged itself free of Ivor's grasp. *"Bottom!"* he yelled. "Half fathom bottom."

Angus shouted to the rowers to feather their oars. Ivor raised his and, at the next dip, plunged it down.

"Wading depth!" The beach was shoaling fast. He scanned the beach, which looked like shingle, not sand, but there were no rocks in sight.

"Ship oars!" Angus shouted. "Bring her in!"

On the next dip, the keel struck. Ivor staggered. Everyone but Angus and Ivor leaped over the gunwale into the icy ocean. *Saints, but that water must be cold!* Rowers' strong hands grabbed the ship and lifted, dragged, and worked it farther up the beach with each wave until it was secure. Then Ivor lifted the grapnel, not without difficulty, and heaved it overboard to Dermid Mór—Dermid the Big—who grabbed it as if it weighed nothing, and ran it up the strand while Ivor paid out the line. There being no handy rock to act as a bollard, Dermid buried the grapnel in the shingle.

Then Ivor could jump ashore also, but he waited until the next wave washed up, to show that he didn't care if he got wet too, although the water barely reached his ankles. Yes, it was freezing.

"To arms!" Angus had seen the lights approaching. Men scrambled aboard again to fetch swords and shields. Having no weapon except the dagger hung on his belt, Ivor just stood were he was and shivered. There should be no danger on the holy island; monks did not fall on visitors with violence. Yet there was something uncanny about a welcome party being on the spot at this hour. *Sea Eagle* carried no lights. It was hard to believe that watchers ashore could have seen it before it rounded the cape, only minutes ago.

This might not be the holy isle.

Four men, not three. Three carried flaming torches, and one a wooden cross. By the time they came trudging across the shingle, it was clear that they were no army, no threat to twenty-one Glenbroch swordsman and one half-frozen Glenbroch boy. Ivor did not even try to push himself forward. To do anything but wait at the back would be stupid bravado; he was unarmed, he was the one who bore the mormaor's message. It made perfect sense. So why did he feel like a coward, hiding behind the swordsmen?

The monks halted. They wore robes and beards, and even

the light of their torches revealed nothing about the men themselves except the glint of their eyes.

"Welcome to the holy island in the name of Jesus Christ, Our Lord," intoned the one with the cross. Moonlight streaked his beard with silver.

"We thank you and we come in peace," Angus replied as his men hastily sheathed their swords. "We are men of Alba, under the orders of Mormaor Malcolm of Stiegle. I am Angus of Glenbroch."

"Blessings upon you, Angus," the monk said with a hasty gesture. "But time is short. Bring forth the wingéd boy."

"The what?" Angus said, at a loss for once.

"The wingéd boy you carry. The holy abbot would speak with him."

There was only one person present who could be described as a boy, wingéd or not, and more than cold was making his teeth chatter now. What was going on?

Angus said, "Oh!" and turned around to look at the company. Men cleared out of the way, until Ivor stood alone, all eyes upon him. He raised his chin defiantly—which helped keep his teeth better-behaved—and stalked forward.

He bowed. "I am Ivor of Glenbroch, runner for the mormaor."

"I am Prior Tuathal. Come with me, Ivor." He turned and began to walk.

"Wait, Prior!" Angus boomed. "We are in need of water and victuals."

The prior turned. Although he was a tall man, he was shorter and slighter than Angus. His title implied that he was the abbot's deputy, but his attitude stated clearly that he knew who was in charge here. He pointed into the darkness. "Fill your barrels at yon burn; it flows sweet water. When the sun rises, take a wether."

"Two, if you please. We shall pay for the beasts."

"They are free, for holy charity, but you may make a donation to the monastery if you please. Come, boy!" Prior Tuathal set off again.

Ivor glanced at Angus and the rest of the crew. They all looked as puzzled as he felt, and perhaps awed. There couldn't be any danger here, could there?

And what if there were? Ninian always insisted that a runner must display confidence—confidence in his ability to repeat his message perfectly, confidence in its importance, and confidence in the custom that messengers were never harmed or punished for bringing bad news.

So Ivor just dipped his chin in a nod of thanks to the sailors for bringing him to this appointment, then raised it again as he strode off after the monks, with his wet cloak flapping around his ankles.

Chapter 5

Prior Tuathal stalked across the beach with one of the torch-bearers at his side to guide him. Ivor found himself flanked by another, while the third brought up the rear. His companion was invisible inside his cowl, but seemed young, being quite short and moving nimbly.

What in Heaven was going on? If this were a trap and the monks were bandits disguised, surely the first person they should try to decoy away would be Angus, to leave his men leaderless? But that theory made no sense either. Nobody back in Stiegle had known that *Sea Eagle* would visit the holy island. Probably only Malcolm himself had known even to what point of the compass it was headed, or who was going to receive the chest of silver. If he had wanted Ivor to call in at Eyin Helga, he would have said so. And *Sea Eagle* had made such fast time that it could not have been expected.

No, there had been some horrible mistake. Ivor wondered what would happen if he removed his cloak and smock to show that he did not possess the tiniest trace of wings, not a feather. But in places the path was steep enough that being wingéd would be a good idea.

"I'm Ivor."

The monk flipped back his hood. "I am Brother Peadar." He was little older than Ivor. His face was gaunt, his beard showed like patches of moss on a rock, his tonsured scalp needed a shave. His smile seemed friendly enough, although it displayed very protuberant teeth.

The path soon became a faint trail through coarse grass and rocks, almost impossible terrain in moonlight, especially for bare feet, but the monks were barefoot also, so Tuathal could not go fast, despite his impatience. The smelly torches had to be held low in order to shed much light on the ground at all; they also sparked, so the three ranks were staying well apart. That pompous, puffed-up prior would not hear anything Peadar told Ivor.

"How many people live on the island?"

"Just we brothers—fourteen of us now. Once there were many more of us, and crofter families also, but they were all taken by the Northmen, or have fled in terror of them."

"It must be a lonely life." Ivor tried not to let his horror show in his voice.

"That is why we chose it. Here we are not tempted by the evils of the world."

True. Some of those evils might be going to catch up with Ivor of Glenbroch very soon. Would Eyin Helga then seem like a better choice?

"I don't have wings, you know. None at all."

Peadar's smile broadened. "The saint often speaks in allegories."

"Saint?"

"Abbot Seumas is a very holy man, a saint."

"I thought only dead people could be saints."

"No, no, no! Many saints are honoured in their lifetimes for the miracles they perform. Anyway, Abbot Seumas is very close to the end of his earthly labours. He insists that he must speak with you first."

"He performs miracles?" Ivor was a good Christian. Why should he find it hard to believe in a holy man who could do that in these modern times?

"Oh yes. Tonight he knew you were coming and where you would land."

Hmm... Well, in that case maybe there really was something important going on. "But if he knew I was coming, why doesn't he know what I came here to tell him?"

"You do not know what he will tell you!" Peadar flipped his hood forward and did not answer Ivor's next three questions.

The sound of the surf had faded. The going became easier and flatter, as they crested the little hill and began following a path between carved stones, but the moon had taken refuge in a cloud. Ivor guessed that he was walking through a graveyard.

"Is this where the kings are buried?"

"No," Peadar said without raising his hood. "These were monks, like me."

Like him, but dead. Ivor still felt that death might be an improvement over life on this lonely, treeless rock.

The moon sprang out from cover, shining behind a high stone cross, an imposing silhouette, but also clearly lighting one on the other side of the path. It stood at least ten feet high, and every inch of its surface—on the upright, the arms, and the circle supporting the arms—was intricately carved. But one of the arms had been broken away.

"Sacrilege!"

Peadar stopped and held up his torch to let Ivor study the wrecked monument. "Northmen's work. Many times they came here, stealing, killing, torturing monks to make them reveal where the treasures were buried, even though their fathers and grandfathers had stolen all the treasures years before. And they will come again, the holy abbot has said."

"I thought the Northmen were Christians now?"

"When they want to be," said a harsh growl—Tuathal had returned to see what the delay was. "And Satan's devils when they want to be. You will see what else they did when the sun rises. Once this holy place was famed throughout Christendom for its art and learning. Men came from many lands to study and worship here. Now only memories and a few monks remain."

"And some famous dead," Ivor said brashly.

"Famous? There are many kinds of fame, not all to be admired. The holy relics were long ago removed to safety. The bones of dead kings remain. This grave over here..." He moved a few yards along the path. "...is the resting place of Donald. Now stop wasting time and do as I say."

Ivor had been born in the reign of King Donald, Constantine's cousin and predecessor, but he was given no time to offer a prayer, for Prior Tuathal was still moving. Soon they left grave markers and passed by what Ivor took at first to be a pile of rocks, padded with turfs. That was exactly what it was, but someone inside was mumbling prayers, so it was also a monk's cell. An owl swooped overhead, white in the moonlight. Then past more heaps, all silent... Tuathal left the path and stopped after ten or twelve yards, near where a faint light showed from yet another pile of rocks.

"The saint is very frail now," he said softly, "and near to his passing. But his hearing is still good, so you do not have to shout at him. Listen carefully to his blessed words. You are honoured to have this chance, boy."

Shivering, Ivor would have preferred to settle for the rest of his night's sleep and a good breakfast, but he said, "Yes, Father."

Tuathal bent down by the entrance. "Brother Flann?"

The sack or blanket that covered the mouth of the kennel was pushed aside to reveal a tonsured scalp. Another monk crawled out on hands and knees and stood up.

"He is sleeping, Father."

Tuathal handed over his cross for safe keeping and disappeared inside. Ivor heard the low drone of his voice, but no reply. In a moment he scrabbled out again, feet first.

"You will go in now, Ivor."

Thinking of numerous things he would rather be doing, Ivor knelt down and crawled under the smelly blanket into the stinking kennel. There was barely enough room for a visitor to sit, certainly not to lie down or stand up. Light came from a tallow candle perched on a rock, and its reek contributed part of the overall stench, being aided by those of rot, urine, vomit, and ancient sweat. In combination, they would gag a goat.

Most of the floor space was occupied by a sleeping platform, about a hand high, on which lay the dying abbot, mostly covered by a fur. His face had shrunk to the shape of a skull and was the same corpse colour as his wispy beard. His mouth hung open, showing a few stumps of teeth; his eyes were wide and seemed to be filled with milk. The only miracle in sight was that he had not been buried weeks ago.

What to say? "Your blessings on a sinner, Holiness."

The blind eyes turned in his direction. After a moment he said, "Ivor of Bracken." His voice was barely a whisper, but clearly to speak at all was a huge effort for him.

"Aye." At the beach Ivor had given Prior Tuathal his new name, Ivor of Glenbroch. Back home, he and his brothers had been known as sons of Bracken because their great-grandfather had farmed a steading of that name up the glen, but that name meant nothing to outsiders. How had this relic known him by it? Yet Ivor somehow still felt deep inside that he was Ivor of Bracken, especially now, after the reunion on *Sea Eagle*. "I have come, Father."

A skeletal arm extended a very shaky hand in his direction. He drew a deep breath and reluctantly leaned forward until it made contact with his face. Dry fingertips traced out his forehead, eyebrows, nose, and so on, like a spider walking down his face. At last it was withdrawn.

"Yes," the old man murmured, as if he recognized Ivor. "I have seen you..." His voice was so soft that Ivor had to lean very close.

"What are you telling me, Father?"

"Seen... you have destiny. At the wolf's house... You must turn the spear!" His breath would petrify a basilisk and he was the source of much of the stink. Soap and clean linen were not allowed by vows of poverty; filth and lice were understood to be part of the religious life.

"I am to go to the wolf's house? You mean Dunfaol? And..."

But Seumas was speaking again. "...the box?"

How did he know about the box? All Ivor's suspicions flared up anew, like embers caught by a sudden draft. "It's safe on the ship, Holiness."

"Bring... church... must bless it... at sext... go... sleep now."

Again the hand rose. Again Ivor offered his face. This time the spider walked up his face and came to rest on his hair. He heard a faint mumble of a blessing: "... *et fillii et Spiritus Sancti.*"

The hand sagged back and papery lids closed on blind eyes, as if the old man had exhausted the last of his energy. The audience was over. Ivor tucked Seumas's arm under the fur and adjusted the rug to cover him better. Then he backed out into the fresh air and clambered to his feet.

He sucked in several deep breaths. Already the world was brightening under a colourless sky. The long summer dawn might tarry a while yet, but now there was enough light to show a horizon. He looked around at the ruined landscape, dominated by the remains of a church, surrounded by broken crosses and some rubble that might once have been other buildings. There was not a tree in sight. To the east towered hills that must be mainland, or the next island, for Eyin Helga was a tiny place. The four monks were waiting for him.

"You heard the holy one's message?" Tuathal demanded.

"I think... Yes. But I didn't understand all—"

The prior raised a surprisingly large hand. "Do not ask me or anyone else to explain. The message was for you, and the meaning will be revealed to you when needed. In our own lack of understanding, we might give you wrong guidance."

So what "turning the spear" meant would have to wait until later. Thorfinn Fleinn, Thorfinn the spear...

Brother Flann had dropped on all fours to return to his vigil over the patient.

"The abbot told me he was going to sleep now," Ivor said. "And he wants me to bring, um, a package up from the ship so he can bless it—at sext, he said." That much had been clear enough. "In the church. It's too big to fit in his cell."

Evidently his words were welcome, for even the dour prior brightened.

Peadar murmured, "He must be feeling stronger," and was frowned at for speaking unbidden.

"Then we shall expect you and your package at noon," Tuathal announced. "Your companions, also, in the Lord's name. Meanwhile, Ivor, you are welcome to join us in morning prayers and then break your fast with us."

The monks probably lived on oatmeal, with a few beans and dandelion leaves when they were lucky. Down on the shore, *Sea Eagle*'s crew would have caught their sheep and started roasting them.

"I thank you, but I had better go reassure the sailors, Father Prior. They were alarmed to be met when our coming had not been announced. I'm sure they will return with me at noon." Ivor could not imagine himself carrying that box of silver up the hill singlehanded. He beat a hasty retreat.

Chapter 6

As he picked his way down the path he tried to make sense of the old man's words. *Wolf's house* was easy. *Faol* meant a wolf, and *dun* a fort, so the wolf's house was Ragnvaldr's stronghold, Dunfaol. In any case, that was the logical place to start looking for him—or his successor, if Ragnvaldr himself had met with a political misfortune.

Turning the spear, though, was as clear as slate. He could ask Jock the Brain. Or Angus. Angus had always been head of the family, his substitute father. Their father, the senior Ivor of Bracken, had died before Ivor was born, and their mother when he was ten.

No, he mustn't ask Angus. Now he understood Malcolm's orders that he was not to take *Sea Eagle*'s crew into his confidence. They had not heard the mormaor's explanation, and to present them with a puzzle like Seumas's prophecy would result in an enormous argument and twenty different answers. To involve even Angus would be unfair, for the safety of his crew must be his prime concern. So it came back to Ninian's insistence on a show of complete confidence. The Glenbroch men—yes, even Angus—would be much happier if they believed that their noble passenger knew exactly where he was going and what he was doing. Ivor had been given the job. Ivor wore the king's ring. He was their leader, and a leader must never admit to doubts.

Most of the crew were still asleep on the grass, cocooned in their cloaks, but a few were up, gathering driftwood for a fire. No doubt others had gone off with bows to shoot breakfast. The tide had gone out. It would be possible to launch the ship now, but not without a lot of hard work.

Angus came striding out to accost Ivor, eyes searching his face for traces of worry. "All right?"

"Very impressive! He knew me! He'd had some sort of a vision of me arriving. A nightmare, I expect."

"No doubt."

The joke had been a mistake, suggesting nervousness. "He's a very holy man, older than the hills. I have to take that chest of mine up to the church at noon to receive his blessing."

"I expect you'd like some help with that," the big man said. "And after?"

"After that we go to Dunfaol to find the Lord of the Isles."

Angus nodded. "We'd better be loading up with roast mutton, then."

He knew Ivor too well to be fooled by Ivor's bravado, but he wasn't going to call his bluff.

▶▼◀

Having no claims to be a cook, Ivor lent a hand gathering driftwood and scrub for the fire. The pickings were lean, because the monks had been there first, but there was a good blaze going by the time the hunters returned. The sheep on the island were feral, abandoned when their owners had fled or been slain. One ram had tried to charge Tomas, to everyone's amusement. It tasted good.

Ivor was almost finished his second slab, with grease all over his hands and chin, when he saw a robed figure approaching, soon recognizable as Peadar. He rose and went to greet the visitor.

The monk smiled diffidently. "Brother, I beg a kindness. As you know, the saint is very frail and has not even visited the church in almost a month. Attending the sext service will be a strain on him... We are not allowed meat, except when sick, but if you could spare a piece, just enough to make a broth for him...?

"Certainly," Ivor said, and led him back to the group to be introduced. While Dermid was hacking off a shank, Ivor saw a chance to bolster the crew's enthusiasm for the coming effort of carrying the heavy treasure chest up the hill. "Recount for us some of the miracles the holy one has performed in the past."

Peadar flashed him an amused glance, as if guessing roughly what he was up to, and showed his jumble of teeth in a smile. "Truly, they are wonderful! He has calmed storms many times, and raised the sick. He berated a gang of ferocious Northmen raiders until they wept for shame and begged forgiveness. Most wonderful of all, a drowned sailor was washed ashore on this very beach once, and the abbot breathed in his mouth and brought him back to life!"

"Praise the Lord!" Ivor said. If Seumas's breath had been one-half as vile then as it was now, a corpse could be excused for trying to get away from it. The crew mostly looked impressed, though. "You are welcome to join us in our feast, Brother."

The young monk sighed regretfully. "My vows forbid it, but I thank you for your offer." He accepted the meat for the abbot, blessed the crew, and headed off, back up the hill.

Ivor scurried after him to walk at his side. "Brother, why me? Why did the abbot want me, and if you're going to say that it is God's will, then why is it God's will? Why am I so special?"

Peadar showed his terrible teeth again.

"Never question the Lord's will, Ivor! Kings like to fight, but only God determines who wins. Sometimes it seems to us mortals that he has made a very strange choice, but we must take his decisions on faith, for he knows all, and we know nothing. He seems to see you as a worthy servant to bear whatever burden he will lay upon you. Obey humbly and all will be well, if not in this world, then in the next."

Ivor thought, *See you there, then*, but he just said, "Thank you, Brother," and went back to finish breakfast.

▶▼◀

No miracles were revealed at the service, which turned out to be almost commonplace. The struggle to recover the chest from under the gratings and lift it down to the beach had been more exciting, costing two crushed fingers and some badly bruised ribs when Fergus tripped over an oar and fell against the gunwale. The load was well bound to two oars to act as poles, and Angus divided the crew into teams of four by height, to take turns at carrying the monster. Even those strapping rowers found the work hard. Ivor thought he ought to share it, but Angus forbade that. A runner with a hernia or a dislocated shoulder would not be worth delivering anywhere, he said, and he was in charge of transportation matters.

The church must have been impressive once, although probably dark inside, for its walls were thick and its windows small; originally they had been glazed with a fretwork of lead and many-coloured glass, of which only traces remained. Now, with the roof gone and much of the east end collapsed, the summer sun shone in, weeds and thistles grass grew in the nave. Carvings had been battered, pillars had fallen. The altar was a plain stone slab supported on two other slabs, like a small table. Its candlesticks were made of coarse pottery.

The church would never have held more than fifty people and seemed quite crowded when twenty visitors were packed in among the ruins, sitting on fallen stones, planks, or even in the weeds. The seating seemed almost haphazard, except that the monks ended mostly east of the altar and the sailors west of it. Ivor was annoyed to find himself set apart from his friends, alongside Brother Peadar, who seemed to have been given the chore of sheep-dogging the laymen, or perhaps just him.

"This must have been beautiful," the monk said sadly, "when Saint Callum built it. Kings and nobles brought it many glorious and precious things, but they were all stolen by Ingvarr the Tusk, or by those who came after him."

"Perhaps I'll see some of those treasures when I get to Dunfaol."

"Perhaps, but asking for them back won't get you far. I have another favour to ask, Ivor. Will you let me come along with you? The prior told me to ask you."

"What on earth for?"

"Because it is important to record the lives and deeds of holy men like Seumas. I am anxious to witness the good fortune his blessings will bring you."

So was Ivor of Glenbroch.

"There isn't much room on the ship, but I'll ask Angus. The decision will have to be his."

"He seems like a good man," Peadar said, as happily as if he had been given a promise. "I am from the north, so I may be some help with the language. Not much, I fear, for my parents brought me south when I was a child, but perhaps better than none."

Ivor found the young monk's humility quite touching,

and very different from the braggart self-assurance of the housecarls who made up *Sea Eagle*'s crew.

When everyone else was ready, Abbot Seumas was brought in, moving very slowly and supported by Prior Tuathal and Brother Flann. He was guided to a wooden chair near the altar. They had made some effort to dress him up, comb his beard, shave his scalp, and he seemed more alert than he had when Ivor say him earlier. He scanned around until he located Ivor, and smiled toothlessly in his direction—which would have been unremarkable, except that the old man was quite obviously stone-blind.

The monks sang a hymn, a well-known one, so the visitors could join in. The prior said Mass. And then, alarmingly, the abbot struggled to his feet, aided by the prior and Brother Flann, and stepped close to the altar. Tuathal removed the candles and nodded a signal. Four monks came forward to lift the treasure box.

This, Ivor decided, was going to be interesting. Aside from chores like gardening, the holy men lived sedentary lives; they fasted often and ate sparingly of a vegetarian diet. Alas, they could not compete with rowers' muscles. One end of the box stubbornly refused to rise at all. The other did lift a few inches, and was quickly set down again.

Angus rose and nodded to Aidan and Dermid—and Ivor, to Ivor's alarm. If he did no better than the monks he would never live it down. The monks withdrew, the four Glenbroch men took their place. The chest was raised and laid on the altar. Fortunately the altar was low, for Ivor doubted that he could have lifted his corner any higher. He went back to his place beside Peadar, who was clearly having trouble keeping a straight face.

The box was larger than the altar it sat on, but seemed quite steady. Old Seumas stretched out his shaky hands until he located it, then raised his voice for the first time in Ivor's experience. It was a croaky, quavering voice, but quite audible in the little church, and no doubt also to God, whom he addressed.

The blessing was brief, but the Latin was beyond Ivor's comprehension, although he heard the usual *Patris et fillii et Spiritus Sancti*, and something that sounded like *Ivorum Brakenni*. The prior seemed worried by something the abbot said, though, and glanced at a couple of the older monks. And Brother Peadar's eyebrows had risen. Everyone said Amen.

"What did he say wrong?" Ivor whispered.

"Nothing."

"Tell me or I won't let you have a ride in my boat!"

The monk glanced at him, saw that he was joking, and returned a small smile. "He blessed the *arcam*, which means the chest, not the contents. It doesn't matter. He may not even know what those are, but the blessing is still valid. And he did ask God to protect you from evil on your travels."

Ivor found himself oddly comforted by that news.

Sea Eagle left the holy island at dawn the next day, with the monk aboard.

Chapter 7

Eyin Helga marked the northermost limit of Alba on the west coast. Beyond that lay the domain of the Lord of the Isles, consisting of many islands and much mainland also. Neither Angus nor any of his men had raised any objection to taking on Brother Peadar as another passenger. As far as they were concerned, Ivor was approved by the mormaor, by the king, and now by God, so whatever he wanted was perfectly acceptable. Ivor was certain that they would all meet with a drastic disappointment within the next day or two. He hoped they would survive it, because he suspected that none of them would.

The weather had become less cooperative, as if to demonstrate that *Sea Eagle* could no longer rely on Ireland to protect it from the spite of the world ocean, for west of them now lay nothing but water, unless one counted legendary places like Hy-Brasil, Tír na nÓg, and Iceland. Angus chose to stay within sight of the coast, but the wind blew stubbornly from the northwest, so he could not raise the sail and the men had their work cut out rowing in the heavy swell. They found a quiet sea loch to overnight in, a place with a tongue-twister name, whose inhabitants were grudgingly hospitable. They were willing to sell the visitors food at outrageous prices, but offered no shelter. Brother Peadar went ashore to confer with the priest, and returned to report that the good man had heard no news of political troubles.

The next morning troubles found *Sea Eagle*. Two longships came into view astern, and it was a very safe bet that they were not Alban. Possibly *Sea Eagle* had been sighted and the Northmen were giving chase, but it seemed more likely that they were just heading in roughly the same direction and were faster, because after a while they changed course to come to investigate. On a coast so indented, there was no reason why the visitors could not have passed by a Northmen's settlement without seeing it.

Ivor sat on the gratings in the bow with his chin on his knees and worried about what to do now. He had reached a decision point: did he announce himself as a messenger sent by Mormaor Malcolm or by King Constantine? Buckle or ring? Malcolm had given him the right to define his mission either way, and normally there would be no argument, for a royal message would carry a lot more weight. But the Lord of the Isles claimed royal honours for himself, and Constantine's claim of overlordship was a polite fiction at best. If the earl chose to do so, he could take offence and order Ivor's head cut off—but he could do that even if he just disliked the shape of his eyebrows.

Eventually he decided there was no way he could make a valid decision, so he should leave the matter up to chance. Or God. Besides, he was neglecting his duties as water boy. He rose and walked carefully between the two ranks of sweating rowers, all the way to the stern, where Angus and Brother Peadar sat.

"Tanist, do you have an Alban flag aboard?" he asked.

The ship was flying the Mormaor's colours.

Angus raised his bushy brows. "Aye, that we do."

"Then pray raise it."

"Hold this," his brother said.

Brother Peadar jumped up to make room on the bench for Ivor to sit and take the steering oar. Angus went to find the flag. The monk sat down again and waited until Ivor picked up the stroke with the mallet before he spoke.

"Why are you doing that? You think they love King Constantine more than they love Mormaor Malcolm?"

"I think they may fear him a little more." Ivor was guessing that Malcolm thought the same, for why else would he have given him leave to speak in the king's name? He had only a hunch to go on, and his neck to gamble.

Angus ran the royal flag up the mast and returned to the stern. As he took the helm again, he asked, "What do I say when we're challenged?"

"That the water boy gets to speak first," Ivor said grumpily, and went to do his duties with a canteen.

It was now clear that the two longships were intent on intercepting *Sea Eagle* and had a better turn of speed, so eventually Angus turned the bow into the swell and ordered the oars shipped. In about fifteen minutes, the leading ship of the pair came in close and hove to. The vessels rocked in unison, with the longer vessel clearly more stable.

"This is where you do some work and the rest of us get to watch, Runt," Angus said. He was smiling, but his eyes were full of concern for this fledgling of his now launched into the real world.

"About time, I'd say." Ivor smiled back, but looking confident was not so easy when you were scared out of your wits.

The longship's master was a huge red-bearded man, nearly as big as Angus and sounding a lot more aggressive.

He needed no bullhorn to make himself heard, although his Norse accent made him hard to understand.

"Identify yourselves, strangers."

Ivor rose to answer, which must have surprised him. "I am Ivor of Glenbroch, runner for Malcolm of Stiegle, but I bear a message to the Lord of the Isles from King Constantine."

"Couldn't he have sent a grown man, instead of a wee bairn?"

"Size is no proof of worth. What's your name, Goliath?"

"I'm Thane Hector of Gark, and I'll stand for none of your sassing. Gi'e me the message and I'll see it's delivered."

Curiously, Ivor suddenly discovered that he was enjoying this. Fifteen feet of cold ocean between him and the giant certainly helped, but any action was better than just brooding.

"I can't. I must deliver it in person to the Lord of the Isles."

"*King of the Isles*. Which one?"

"How many have you got?"

"Och, just one, but there's some discussion about what his name is."

Although Ivor dared not take his eyes off Thane Hector, he sensed that both crews were enjoying the exchange. Just pray that it remained verbal...

"You on your way to help settle the matter?"

"If it isn't settled before we get there."

"Why don't we follow you in, and I'll give my message to the last man standing?"

"You were made a messenger because your mouth's so big?"

Angus cleared his throat. That made a very small noise, almost inaudible under the sound of the water lapping on the hull, and the creak of rope and timber as the ships rocked, so likely only Ivor and Peadar were close enough to hear it. What it suggested was that, while witty backtalk was entertaining commoners, and especially juvenile commoners, who lipped a Northman thane were liable to experience the sort of splitting headache that only a battleaxe could create. Ivor understood the message.

He said, "It's all I've got, my lord. I wouldn't dare challenge you to arm wrestling."

"Who's the big lunk beside you?"

Angus stood up. "I'm his brother, Tanist Angus of Glenbroch. I'll look after any arm wrestling he needs done." A tanist, heir-apparent to a thane, carried much more weight than a mere runner. Ivor had often been told that he resembled Angus, and now that they were the same height, their likeness was probably even clearer.

"We'll discuss that at Dunfaol," the thane said. "Three hours, if that southern rabble of yours can row as well as honest northerners."

"Never met one of those," Angus said. "But try for two hours, I'm thirsty." He sat down and reached for the steering oar. *Sea Eagle*'s rowers were grinning and giving the brothers thumbs-up signs. That felt good, but the Northmen's glowers were promising Ivor at least a vicious beating as soon as his mission to the earl was completed.

▶▼◀

The little flotilla set off, with Thane Hector's ship in the lead and the other Northmen following close behind *Sea Eagle*. With their larger crews, they could afford to set a mean pace, and did.

"So Ragnvaldr Leifrson is being challenged?" Angus said. "That surprise you?"

It was time to confess. "No. The mormaor warned me that the Isles were unstable. He thought that the upstart was a scoundrel called Thorfinn Fleinn. I was hoping it would be settled before we arrived. It looks like we may be heading into a real nastiness."

Angus glanced briefly at Brother Peadar, who must have guessed what was in that so-heavy chest.

"And who gets the mormaor's gift, Runt?"

"Um... That's up to me to decide."

The tanist groaned. "You'd better make the right choice."

What he didn't say, but Mormaor Malcolm had hinted, was that there might be enough silver in that box to buy half the thanes in the Isles. If the issue were still in doubt, Ivor should be able to swing the victory to whichever contender he chose, with the loser ending up in chains at best, and a grave more likely. If Thorfinn Fleinn was indeed the challenger, Ivor might then have turned the spear—away from Ragnvaldr Leifrson and Alba.

Brother Peadar had been listening, of course. "And which side do you want to choose, Ivor?"

"The winning one," the runner said glumly.

▶▼◀

The nastiness that Ivor had predicted looked even nastier an hour or so later, when two more longships joined their flotilla. The Northmen crews shouted back and forth in their guttural Norse tongue, which even Brother Peadar claimed he could barely understand; he refused to venture any guesses about what was being said. Thane Hector seemed to be accepted as the overall leader.

Four ships, all apparently heading to Dunfaol, were too many to be just a chance meeting. There must be a lot more heading that way, and when the fleet entered the sea loch that was their destination, that guess was fully confirmed. Dozens of ships of various sizes were already pulled up on the beach, all lying like basking seals with their snouts inland and their tails in the water, or like a catch of fish threaded through their gills. Another six were coming in, not counting *Sea Eagle*'s and its escort.

"If this is a coup we've fallen into," Angus said, "they ought to be fighting it out before our very eyes, and I see no sign of that. The decision must have been made."

"Or it isn't a coup," Ivor countered unhappily. "Ragnvaldr Leifrson promised Malcolm that he would make no war this summer, just send his young hotheads to beat up some Irish. But I'm seeing a whirling big beginners' class."

"It's two thousand men at least, maybe three."

Malcolm's fleet had mustered at Abtaraig Bay, now the Northmen's fleet was mustering at Dunfaol.

"This smells of treachery," Ivor told Angus. "Earl Ragnvaldr sent his son Snorri to Stiegle as a hostage. So either he has gone back on his word, or he has been betrayed, for this certainly looks like a muster for war, and Alba's as likely a target as Ireland."

He had spoken softly, but Brother Peadar had heard. "I'm still not sure," he said, "but it's possible that the coup has not yet happened. I can hear men shouting about both Ragnvaldr and Thorfinn."

"Please stay as close as you can to me when we go ashore," Ivor told him. "If you learn that Ragnvaldr is still the earl, then say, 'Saints be praised!', and if it's Thorfinn say, 'Hallelujah!'."

"And if it's anyone else," Angus suggested, "recite the prayers for the dead."

▶ ▼ ◀

Dunfaol Glen was wider than Glenbroch, and flanked by mountains much higher than its gentle hills. There were cottages down by the beach, but most of the population must live in the fort, which stood on an isolated hill about half a mile inland. To Ivor's untutored eye it looked much more formidable than Stiegle.

Thane Hector's ship veered close. "Glenbroch!" the big man roared. "You beach alongside me and keep your rabble on board while I report to the king. We don't want any accidents do we? The fun can start later."

Angus shouted. "Aye for now, but we're short of water."

The thane replied with an obscene suggestion, and shouted to his coxswain to steer for the widest gap he could see. Obeying instructions, Angus followed. Once *Sea Eagle* had been dragged ashore, flanked on either side by one of Hector's ships, the Albans clambered back aboard with an ill grace. There could be no escape, at least not by daylight, and sunset was still some hours away.

Every skipper leading his crew ashore posted pickets to guard his ship; Hector of Gark left more men than most, to keep watch on the strangers also. *Sea Eagle*'s weary sailors shared out their food and water and prepared to wait upon events.

Brother Peadar, though, clambered ashore without asking leave of anyone. He was at once accosted by one of Hector's swordsman, hand on hilt. The monk calmly blessed him; perhaps he also reminded him of what God did to men who took up arms against his servants, for after a moment the Northman stepped aside and let Peadar go on his way.

▶▼◀

Angus sat in the bow to eat his meal, for trouble must come from the beach when it came, as come it certainly would. Ivor joined him, but then Fergus, Jock, Lachlan, and Tomas crowded in on them for a family reunion. That in itself was pleasant, except that it felt as if they were defending Ivor from the rest of the crew, so as soon as he had finished eating, he slipped through between them and went to speak with the others. Not wanting to shout, he knelt and spoke with them in small groups, explaining that he had been sent with a message of good will to Earl Ragnvaldr, but now it looked as if the earl had either gone back on his word to Mormaor Malcolm, or had been deposed. Inevitably he was then asked what happened next, and each time he replied that he had brought enough silver to buy their way out of it.

Which was probably not true.

When he returned to the bow, Angus asked if he wanted the money chest brought out. Ivor said he would rather wait and see what the situation was. Once the box was revealed it could not be hidden again.

Eventually Brother Peadar came scrambling back aboard. He did not look happy, chewing his lip with his ragged teeth. "I have news," he said, glancing from Ivor to Angus and back.

Angus's look to Ivor told him he was in charge. *Sea Eagle* had done her job by delivering the ambassador to Dunfaol, so now it was up to the runner to make the decisions. Ivor's belly had tightened like a clenched fist.

"Speak up then," he said.

"Not good. The first thing I heard was a man asking where Ragnvaldr Leifrson was, and the answer was that he was up on the church roof, together with his son Erik and the bishop, but it might be hard to tell them apart now, after the ravens had been working on them for half a day." He made the sign of the cross, and the listeners copied him.

"And the new chief pirate?"

"Thorfinn Fleinn, as you expected. He's been brewing rebellion for months, I gather, all around the Isles, accusing Ragnvaldr of selling out to the Albans. This morning he sailed in with a dozen longships, which was such a show of force that the guards would not even close the fort's gates against him. Thorfinn killed Ragnvaldr with his own hands and claimed the throne."

"Fair fight?" Ivor asked, as if that mattered or was even likely.

"Fair as it could be," Peadar said, "with Thorfinn being

thirty years younger. And he stayed mute when his followers cut down Erik Ragnvaldson like a mad dog."

"So now he's undisputed Lord of the Isles?" Did Snorri Ragnvaldson have a claim to inherit his father's domain? If so, there might still be a loyalist party Ivor could rally with Malcolm's silver. If the Northmen must fight someone this summer, let it be one another!

"Not quite. Bishop Neacel refused to crown him until he confessed and repented of the murders. That explains why he's beside the others on the church roof. There's two other priests, but they've gone into hiding."

"Wish I could," Lachlan said. Jock cuffed his ear.

"Do you really think the lack of the church's blessing will stop a man like Thorfinn?" Ivor asked. He didn't.

"Probably not." Brother Peadar shrugged and headed aft to find a place to sit. There he knelt in prayer and was left undisturbed. His was now the only tonsured scalp in Dunfaol, which no doubt explained why he had his hood up.

"Better bring out the box now," Ivor told Angus. "I've a hunch we're going to need it."

That was easier said than done, for the outgoing tide had left *Sea Eagle* canted over at enough of an angle to make the footing tricky. If dropping the box would have been a dangerous mishap back in Stiegle, it could be catastrophic there, in the heart of what now looked like enemy territory. But after that job was successfully completed and the gratings had been replaced, there was nothing left to do but wait.

Chapter 8

As the sun drew near the western peaks, Thane Hector of Gark came parading along the strand, leading a squad of his men and riding on a very unhappy-looking pony, which probably did not weigh much more than he did. He rode right up to *Sea Eagle*'s bow and looked over the side, surveying the crew with open contempt.

"So who's in charge here now? The man or the boy?"

No doubt this time: Ivor stood up. "I'm the king's messenger, my lord." He held up his thumb to show the ring, although that might mean nothing to a Northman.

The thane spat on the shingle. "There another king up there who's going to eat you raw, kid."

"Not after he's heard what I have to say."

"You're hoping he'll roast you on a spit first? Very well. You come with me, and bring that monk of yours with you."

Ivor had been thinking of Malcolm's words: *When I tried ragging you in the hall, you stood up to me....* That day, which now seemed so long ago, he had been all alone, standing before a man who could have ordered him flogged to raw meat. Now he was facing one who could kill him, but he did have twenty friends and brothers at his back, so any attempt at violence would turn very messy very quickly. The principle was the same: *Stand your ground!*

"Brother Peadar is here as my guest. If you want him, you ask him."

The thane stared at him in disbelief. Probably no one in Gark ever said Boo to him, and the sailors he had left on guard were listening. "When the king's through with you, boy, I'm going to ask for what's left so I can break every bone in your body."

"We're not there yet, though. You're keeping your earl waiting."

Peadar had concluded his prayers and was sitting in the stern, watching proceedings with his cowl down so his tonsure was clearly visible.

"Monk!" Hector bellowed. "King Thorfinn wants you."

"Then I shall answer his call," Peadar said. He rose and began making his way forward.

Ivor hoped his own voice sounded that calm. "I carry a gift for the Lord of the Isles."

"Bring it then," Hector barked.

"It takes four strong men to carry it. Have you serfs, or a horse and cart?"

By that time the sons of Bracken had moved out of the way so the treasure chest was visible.

"That?" Even a lout like Hector would have to be impressed by the size of it. But he must also see that bringing a box of bullion before the king instead of just a bigmouthed upstart youth was going to reflect well on him.

"That," Ivor confirmed. "I shall need four men with me to

carry it and four more to spell them off. Twelve in all would be better and faster. Yes, twelve."

"Just you and the monk. I'll have a couple of my lads carry it for you."

"No, my lord. Until I have presented it to the Lord of the Isles and he has accepted it, it must remain in Alban hands. And my companions will be armed," Ivor added recklessly. He stopped himself before he started babbling that Northmen were notorious pirates and cattle thieves.

A purple vein stood out on the thane's forehead. "I've warned you about that mouth of yours before, boy."

Malcolm had said, *You glared furiously and still didn't crumble.* Ivor was trying to glare, but he was very close to losing control of his bladder.

"And I've warned you that you are wasting your earl's time. Twelve armed men or I stay here and the gift does too. Go and tell Thorfinn that."

"I never make idle threats, boy," Hector said. "Too bad you didn't learn that in time. Have your minions bring the box then, but they won't carry arms into the king's presence."

That was a universal rule, so Ivor said politely, "Thank you, my lord. Detail a bearer party, if you please, Tanist."

▶▼◀

Thane Hector must have realized how absurd he looked straddling the tiny pony with his toes almost touching the ground, so when the procession set off, he led it on foot. Behind him walked a band of his own swordsmen, followed by the treasure chest. As on *Eyin Helga*, it had been lashed to two oars so that four men could share its weight on their shoulders. Then came Ivor of Glenbroch and Brother Peadar, eight spare porters from *Sea Eagle*, and another band of men of Gark. Ivor had no illusions that he was being granted a guard of honour. He was in custody, and that was that.

The shore village was crowded with noisy Northmen wanting food, drink and just plain mayhem. Ivor wondered what had happened to the normal residents, but preferred not to know. He wondered, too, if he would ever see *Sea Eagle* again and the men left to guard it, including Tomas, who was in charge until Angus returned, if he ever did. If the new earl was already determined to make war on Alba, then there was nothing in the world to keep him from killing or enthralling the whole crew and adding the ship to his own fleet. He needn't even say "Thank you" for all the silver.

Possibly Ivor's thoughts showed in his face, for Peadar suddenly said, "Do not loose faith, brother! Remember that holy Saint Seumas blessed your mission."

"It will take a real miracle to get us out of this alive." Ivor could not help remembering that Eyin Helga had been sacked by the Northmen many times, and all the prayers of all the holy men on the island had not stopped that.

"Then a real miracle may be what you will get! Of course," the monk added after a moment, "your life was neither mentioned nor guaranteed. I am confident that your mission will succeed, though. Is that not enough?"

"Yes," Ivor admitted, "that would be enough." He wanted to go on living, but if it came to a choice, he would much rather prevent an attack on Alba. He thought of his enormous extended family still in Glenbroch: brothers, sisters-in-law, nephews, nieces, plus cousins, uncles, and aunts beyond counting; childhood friends. He thought of Stiegle, of Lady Kenina and the beautiful Meg. Maidens like her would suffer more than anyone, for she would become a concubine baby maker to some flea-bitten Northman. The worst that could happen to him would be that he would work out the rest of his life as a serf to one of those, toiling in the fields. Death might be better, as long as it was quick.

The road was busy with sailor-swordsmen coming and going, but they all stood aside to let Hector's party proceed.

The way wound between fields marked out by dry-stone walls, then emerged onto rougher ground as it began to climb the hill. Angus had already changed the bearers twice, and now brought back the first team again, which included himself and Dermid Mór. The Northmen guards jeered at the Alban weaklings.

Ivor had still not decided exactly what message he was going to deliver. It had to be from the king, for he had already told Hector that it would be. But Constantine, or even Malcolm, could not have known to address their words to Thorfinn if the coup had only taken place that morning. So what message could Ivor have been bringing to Ragnvaldr that would be acceptable to the new earl, the self-proclaimed king of the Isles? Any wrong message would get Ivor and his companions killed and Alba attacked, but was there a right message that wouldn't?

He was in no hurry for the journey to end, for life could only get more unpleasant when he arrived at the fort. But end it did, and he followed the chest of Alban silver into Dunfaol, the Wolf's Lair.

The outer wall was high and impressive, the buildings inside mostly built of stone, with steep slate roofs that would protect them from enemies' fire arrows. Ivor had expected his reception by Earl Thorfinn to take place in a hall, but the entire fort seemed to be packed with men, and whatever was happening was happening outdoors on that hot, breathless evening. Some daredevils had climbed up on rooftops to watch. He heard voices speechifying, then cheering, more voices, more cheering.

Hector now demanded that the Alban men relinquish their arms.

"Better still," Ivor said, "why don't they all remain here with the chest, and you take me to speak with the earl."

"The king!"

"His status is what we'll be discussing, but whoever is

in charge here, my message is addressed to him, so let me deliver it."

The big thane showed his fangs in what he probably thought of as a smile. "Good idea. I am really looking forward to what happens after."

Ivor turned to Angus. "Remain and guard that box until we send for you."

"Aye, sir," Angus said. He did not smile but there was a twinkle in his eye. All Ivor's life, Angus had been his father substitute and now he was taking his orders, but that twinkle was approval and encouragement. It might also be farewell.

Ivor's eyes suddenly misted and he spun on his heel.

"Lead on, my lord."

As Hector's men bulled a way through the crowd for them, it became clear that Earl Thorfinn was accepting the respects and allegiance of the assembled thanes. Every speech was much the same and was cheered with equal enthusiasm. The whole bloodthirsty mob was working itself up to make war on Alba. Any thoughts of having sport with the Irish had died with Earl Ragnvaldr, for Alba was a richer prey, offering good loot as well as women and slaves. Everyone knew that Alban warriors were dwarfs, perverts, and cissies.

None of which made a great buildup for a message from the king of Alba. And soon Ivor detected another text below the main one: Ragnvaldr Leifrson had accepted Alban silver and had sent his younger son to Alba for safety, so Ragnvaldr Leifrson had been a traitor. That would not make Ivor's task any easier.

The meeting was being held in a surprisingly large open space in the centre of the fort, possibly meant to serve as a livestock paddock in time of war. The crowd filled and overflowed it. Thorfinn Fleinn was the only man with a seat, indeed a throne, raised up so that he could be seen. He was large, of course, but younger than Ivor had expected, with flaxen hair and bronze beard. His shirt hung open, either because of the heat, or just to let his followers admire his massive furry chest, and he was hatless. Between speeches he would leap to his feet to respond and call forward another of his loyal subjects, and then it could be seen that he wore a sword. He was probably the only man in Dunfaol who did.

He noticed Hector coming, for Hector must have spoken to him earlier, or perhaps it was Brother Peadar's tonsure that caught his eye. He dismissed the current speaker by rising and barking out brief thanks. His command of, "Let Thane Hector approach!" opened the crowd for the three newcomers.

His throne stood in the only open space, a circle fifteen or twenty feet across, enclosed by a solid wall of the largest men, distinguished as thanes by their many golden torcs and arm rings. They stood shoulder-to-shoulder, firmly keeping the rabble out. They were, in a very real sense, the inner circle. Hector thumped a pair of heavy shoulders, and told them to make room. Then he shoved Brother Peadar into the ring ahead of him and took station as part of the human wall. Ivor was left outside it, but he was tall enough to have a good view of proceedings.

At close quarters Thorfinn seemed even larger than Ivor had first thought, for the makeshift platform on which his throne precariously stood was only a large chest, not much more than knee-high. His huge bare feet rested on a footstool before it. He was red-faced, sweaty, and triumphant; undoubtedly deadly.

Thorfinn's words to Brother Peadar were probably the quietest he had spoken in hours. "So, monk, will you set the crown on my head and gabble whatever it is you clerics say on such occasions? I put little stock in your blessings myself, but some of my warriors will kill more happily for me if I have it."

Bishop Neacel had refused and then been martyred. To Ivor's surprise Peadar did not.

"I am not an ordained priest," the monk said calmly, "so I cannot hear your confession and absolve you. But the earl is always elected by his thanes, and as you are obviously in charge here, I will be happy to give you my blessing, for what it is worth."

Ivor just hoped that he could speak as well when his turn came.

Thorfinn's eyes narrowed as he debated that lukewarm reply, but then he nodded. Whatever Peadar said would be in Latin, which nobody else would understand. As long as some sort of cleric said something, most of his thanes would be satisfied, and the rest would know better than to argue. Ivor started breathing again.

"Wait back there," the earl said, gesturing to the space behind his throne. He drank from a flask he held, wiped his beard with a hairy forearm, and turned his gaze on Hector. He raised his voice again, going back to public business.

"Where's this messenger you mentioned?" He was hoarse, but he must have been at this for hours.

Hector turned, grabbed Ivor's arm, dragging him into the circle, and across to the throne. There he hooked one of his feet back and shoved him forward, sending him sprawling, flat on his face in front of the earl's footstool.

"This, Your Majesty."

"That?" Thorfinn roared, although he must have been warned earlier of Ivor's youth. "Constantine has the impudence to send a *boy* to speak with me? Get up, child."

Ivor rose, dusted off his knees, and bowed. "Ivor of Glenbroch, runner to Mormaor Malcolm, sent with a message from the king of Picts and Scots." That might not be technically true, but Malcolm had given him liberty to say whatever he thought was needed, and who was going to live long enough to tell Constantine?

"A message addressed to?"

"To the Lord of the Isles, his mormaor. I was warned that Earl Ragnvaldr might have been replaced by the time I got here."

Thorfinn Fleinn frowned. He was not dealing with his loyal and loving thanes now, and he was being more cautious. "Oh you were? And when did the king tell you that?"

He hadn't. Malcolm had.

"I... I've lost count of days, my lord. About a week ago Mormaor Malcolm dispatched me to His Majesty to tell him that Snorri Ragnvaldson had arrived in Stiegle. That took two days... I left the king's army the following morning, returned to Stiegle, and the next morning boarded a ship to come here."

"So it was Snorri Ragnvaldson who told them that his father was in danger of being deposed?"

"I expect so, my lord. I was not told where the information came from." But the last message Ivor had taken to the king had only told him about Snorri, not that Snorri's father might have sent him south for safekeeping. It was growing harder and harder not to tell an actual lie.

"So what is this message that deserves no worthier messenger than a beardless boy?"

"I also bring a gift, my lord, which is waiting out at the gate. Will you send for it now?"

"What is it? I would welcome nothing you could bring me except Snorri Ragnvaldson's head."

"A box of silver, my lord."

Thorfinn threw back his head and bellowed with laughter. Then he sprang up on the footstool and spoke to his horde: "Did you hear that, my friends? Alba sends me tribute!

He hopes to bribe me as he bribed Ragnvaldr! Well, we'll swallow his silver now to whet our appetites and tomorrow we'll go and eat the rest of the feast, agreed?"

They all agreed, very loudly. Thane Hector had remained beside Ivor, as if to protect the earl from this dangerous maniac he had brought into the fold. He was trying to signal with his hands that it was a very big box, but Thorfinn did not seem to notice.

Or perhaps he did notice and that only made him more determined to emphasize the difference between him and his predecessor. Whatever the truth, he then said something he might shortly regret: "I won't keep the treason money for myself like Ragnvaldr did! Pass the word to the gate to send in this silver and we'll share it out right here and now!" More cheers.

He sat down. "Well, now let's hear the message."

Oh, holy Saint Seumas, if you can send a miracle, send one now!

The ancient abbot had told Ivor to "turn the spear". Surely that meant to turn Thorfinn the Spear aside from attacking Alba? Ivor straightened his shoulders, pressed his palms to his thighs, and spoke up as loudly as he could.

"Constantine II, by the Grace of God, King of the Scots and Picts, Lord of Alba, send greetings to his loyal and beloved Mormaor of the Isles, saying: We send you this token of our love and trust and bid you make all haste to muster your fleet and come south to aid us, your overlord, in our just struggle against the thieves and perverts of Northumbria. Thus spake King Con—"

A massive fist to the side of his head sent Ivor sprawling headlong on the mud.

Chapter 9

Thorfinn, who had risen and begun to draw his sword, sheathed it and sat down again. "We thank you, Thane Hector. I was about to kill a child, which would be a waste of a future serf."

"In this case death would be justified, Your Grace. I did promise him a thorough thrashing as soon as you were finished with him, but I will leave him breathing if you wish it."

"Well, let's see what he brought us. We may decide to be merciful—or we may make him eat it."

Head still spinning from the blow, Ivor struggled to his feet and went to join Brother Peadar at the side of the throne.

"Well done," the monk whispered.

Ivor said nothing. He had bitten his tongue and had blood in his mouth.

Angus and Big Dermid brought in the chest, Angus in

front and Dermid at the rear, and it was obvious that even they were having trouble carrying such a load. The circle of thanes whooped with greedy delight at the sight of it.

"Put it here!" Thorfinn commanded, moving his feet out of the way and pointing at his footstool. That was easier said than done, but the two porters managed it and stepped back.

The footstool uttered a loud groan, as if in agony. Then came a sharp crack and it crumpled under the weight. The box crushed it into a carpet of firewood.

After a moment's hesitation, Thorfinn laughed, so everyone else laughed too. He drew his sword again. "Perhaps I should take that kindling to Constantine and make him eat it? Let us see what he has sent." Leaning forward on his throne, he swung his sword at the ropes binding the box: once, twice, thrice.

At the second blow, Ivor thought he saw the chest move. At the third he was certain of it. That was impossible!

Thorfinn put the tip of his sword under the lid and flipped it off.

The box was empty.

▶▼◀

Brother Peadar was the first to recover the power of speech. "A miracle!" he shouted, amazingly loud. "A blessed miracle! Give thanks to the Almighty and Saint Seumas!" He sank to his knees, hands clasped in prayer.

So did Ivor, although he wasn't sure that he meant to; he might have just collapsed. Angus and Dermid had not yet left the circle; they too copied the monk.

Everyone had seen two large men struggling under the weight of that chest. They had watched it crush a footstool on which the earl himself had been posturing, and he was no lightweight. While Thorfinn might claim to put no faith in the Church's blessing, many of his thanes were Christians and they quickly knelt and made the sign of the cross. In a moment the rest of them did the same, while the massed swordsmen behind them were trying to, but stumbling and struggling in their efforts to find enough room.

Earl Thorfinn was left sitting on his throne, staring in dismay at the wreckage of his hopes. An earl who is made to look such a fool before he has reigned a full day must clearly be cursed. And faith is infectious. Despite his earlier disclaimer of belief in the Church, he had turned very pale above his ruddy beard.

Just in case anyone did not see the importance of what had happened, Peadar stood up and raised his pectoral cross to the earl.

"In the name of Christ Our Lord, Thorfinn, repent!" he shouted. "This miracle has been sent as a warning to you! You are not in state of grace, Thorfinn Fleinn. Your wickedness has offended the Almighty and the gates of Hell are swinging wide to receive your black soul. You must do penance for the murder of three men. You must abjure your evil intentions to make war upon your overlord, King Constantine. I exhort you to mend—"

"No!" Ivor shouted.

He was suddenly certain that the young monk was on the wrong trail. A conjuring trick with a wooden box was never going to persuade Thorfinn to give up his newfound kingship. Nor would he forego his war and just tell everyone, *Sorry, go home now.* Old Saint Seumas had told Ivor to turn the spear, not try to break it. "Be still, Brother. Leave this to me." Ivor stepped forward, took up the discarded lid, and replaced it on the box.

"My lord, you were planning the wrong war! King Constantine sent that silver to his mormaor, and bade him join in his war against the Northumbrians. If you will now swear loyalty to your overlord, as your predecessor did, and obey that command, then surely the Good Lord will withdraw his anger and return the bullion."

He was promising to perform another miracle. Even saints never went that far! They just tried and took the credit later if it worked. If he had guessed wrong, he was a dead man talking.

He dared not take his eyes off the earl to look at Peadar, or Angus, or anyone.

Thorfinn's beard curled in a snarl of disbelief. But he clearly thought he could see a way out of his quandary.

"If I take the oath, you will instantly fill that box with silver, little messenger? You are a saint, to order up miracles?"

"I cannot do that, my lord, but I was directed by the holy Saint Seumas of Eyin Helga, and he can, for he is greatly loved by the Almighty."

"On that condition," the earl said softly, "I will say the words."

"Lend me your cross, Brother Peadar."

Angus was as white as surf, waiting to see his baby brother cut down before his eyes. Ivor accepted the cross from the monk—who looked just as horrified as Angus—and reached across the miracle box to offer it to the earl.

Thorfinn grabbed it but did not raise it for everyone to see, as Ivor had hoped. No matter, this had to be done quickly, before the spell broke or Ivor himself died of terror. And he must keep it as simple as possible.

"Repeat after me: *I, Thorfinn, Lord of the Isles...*"

"I, Thorfinn, Lord of the Isles..."

"*...do solemnly swear...*"

"...do solemnly swear..."

"*...that I will be loyal to my overlord...*"

"...that I will be loyal to my overlord..."

"*...the king of Scots and Picts...*"

"...the king of Scots and Picts..."

"*...and be his man against all his foes.*"

"...and be his man against all his foes."

The moment the earl spoke the final words, the box exploded. Lacking the support of the rope bindings, the sides shattered and fell away, while the lid slithered down a great heap of shining, clattering, clinking silver.

The witnesses all cried out.

Ivor of Glenbroch fainted dead away.

Chapter 10

He could not have been gone for long. He was vaguely aware of someone—almost certainly Angus—carrying him out of the riot that had erupted around the remains of the chest, a mob squabbling ferociously over the silver.

Then he was lying on the mud and someone was slapping his face. His mouth still tasted of blood. He opened his eyes and saw Angus, haggard with worry.

"Stop that," he said. He felt quite lightheaded. "Pick on someone your own size."

Brother Peadar knelt at his other side, murmuring prayers. They were outside the mob, close to the gate. Ivor tried to rise and was pushed back.

"Take your time," Angus said. "Your Holiness."

"And don't start that! It's going to be all right, isn't it?"

"It's more than all right, lad. It's miraculous. Thorfinn is going to lead his fleet against Northumbria, as ordered.

That may mean the plunder will get spread more thinly, but anything is better than the disaster you prevented."

Ivor looked to Peadar, who beamed at him.

"Thank Saint Seumas for me, please?" Ivor said. This time he did sit up. "I only obeyed his orders. I'm hungry!"

▶▼◀

They fed him ample hot meat and plenty of warm beer. Then, in spite of all his protests, Angus and Dermid carried him shoulder high down to the ship. He weighed a lot less than the chest had, they said. The entire crew was ready to worship him, which was absurd and annoying.

Was there anything else he wanted, they asked.

He said no, but he was secretly wishing he'd grabbed a handful of that silver. How much would Malcolm pay a captain of runners who could work miracles on the side?

That was the beer thinking for him.

▶▼◀

Earl Thorfinn wasted no time. A man who has gathered an army of several thousand cannot afford to have it sitting around just eating and drinking. The fleet sailed at dawn, with Captain of Runners Ivor of Glenbroch a reluctant guest aboard the earl's own ship, *Dragonfire*. He had plenty of time for silent prayer during the next week, for he was still much afraid that Thorfinn would change his mind when he got past Eyin Helga and saw the undefended Alban coast.

Amazingly he did not, and one blustery afternoon the Northmen caught up with the Alban forces encamped outside Nilcaster. The town had fallen, because smoke was still rising from the castle, and Malcolm's fleet was lined up along the beach. His camp was probably nearby, hidden behind a line of low sand dunes.

Dragonfire went in alone, flying the Alban flag that Ivor had thought to commandeer from *Sea Eagle*. There could be no doubt that it had been seen, and no doubt Malcolm would be rallying his men to repulse any possible landing. Ivor found himself posted in the bow, right by the dragon figurehead. He felt less like a figurehead himself than a target for archery practice.

Now swordsmen were forming up on the beach, but he thought he could see bowmen behind them. He was on their team, but they didn't know that! The only thing keeping him breathing was that the rest of the fleet was staying out to sea. Then *Dragonfire* caught the surf and began rushing in on her own. Thorfinn bellowed for the crew to ship oars.

A shudder as the keel hit... Ivor vaulted over the side, splashed into the ebbing wave, and began to run forward, waving his arms to show he was unarmed. One of the figures in the rear squirmed through the wall of swordsmen and came racing to meet him. It was Edan, whom he'd last seen in the runners' shed at Stiegle. They shouted each other's names, and slammed together in a hug.

"You're alive! We heard you'd gone north and—"

"It was close," Ivor said. "Earl Thorfinn has brought his whole hird to fight for us. Where's Malcolm?"

"Back at camp... not far."

"Take me."

They ran back to the swordsmen. The commander who broke ranks and strode forward to meet them was Uvan son of Domlech, one of Malcolm's senior housecarls. Of course he knew Ivor.

"Captain of Runners, welcome! Welcome, welcome! You are indeed a sight for sore—" A notoriously talkative senior housecarl.

"I came with Earl Thorfinn, the new Lord of the Isles. He says he's here to fight for the king, but don't turn your back on him yet. I must report to the mormaor."

"Well that's great news for—"

The two young runners were already on their way. They passed through the gap in the now grinning and cheering shield wall, and began to race, first over sand, then the thick, coarse grass of the dunes.

"Why didn't you tell me that morning that you'd been made chief runner in place of Ninian?" Edan asked.

"Because I didn't believe it myself yet. How's the war going?"

"Haven't made anyone rich so far, but we spilled plenty blood, mostly wishy-washy Northumbrian blood."

Then they crested the hill and Ivor saw the Alban army camp about a mile ahead. He hadn't had a good run in ages. He doubled his pace and left Edan standing.

▶▼◀

Again his approach was noted, and a single horseman came cantering out to meet him. As they drew close together, he bellowed, "Ivor!" and reined in, leaping to the ground even before his horse stopped moving. It was Malcolm himself, clad in chain mail and conical helmet.

Ivor halted, puffing a little. He saluted.

"I have a message for you, my lord."

"Speak, then!"

Feet together, shoulders squared, palms on thighs...

"Earl Thorfinn of Dunfaol, Lord and Mormaor of the Isles, sends greetings to Malcolm of Stiegle, Mormaor of the West, prince of Alba, admiral of the fleet, member of the king's council, lord of high justice, and dearly loved brother in Christ, saying: We have come in answer to our royal overlord, King Constantine, to aid his just cause and fight at your side; thus spake Thorfinn of Dunfaol."

The mormaor stared at him for a moment in silence. His eyebrows rose up to hide under the rim of his helmet. Then a smile touched his lips. "Now tell me what he really said."

"My lord, he said, 'Go tell that dung-shoveler, Malcolm, I've come to fight beside him and if I don't get three-quarters of the plunder, I'll take it all.'"

Malcolm bellowed out a laugh. "Oh, Ivor of Glenbroch, you are a miracle worker! I honestly didn't ever believe... Oh, welcome back and thank you!" He grabbed Ivor with both arms and slammed him against his chain mail in a ferocious embrace that drove all the air out of Ivor's lungs.

"My lord," he gasped when he had been released and caught his breath. "Don't trust him too far, will you?"

"Not an inch! But you I trust a million leagues. And here comes Edan. Edan, run back to the shore and tell Earl Thorfinn that he is welcome and just in time for a great battle tomorrow with the ungodly. Explain the situation and suggest that he camp beside the stream over there. Go! Ivor, your entire team is here. Anyone will show you the runners' quarters; I'll get the whole story from you tonight." He vaulted into the saddle and galloped back to his army. Even Ivor couldn't beat that pace over a short distance.

▶▼◀

The runners' billet was one small tent, which already looked crowded and was going to be more so with the addition of the captain, who was determined that if any of them had to sleep under the stars like the common swordsmen, it certainly shouldn't be he. Ilgarach, Gest, and Galan were sitting on the grass outside. They were all older than Ivor and had been longer in Malcolm's service, but none of them showed any sign of jealousy or resentment. They jumped up to hug him, thump his back, offer him beer and congratulations, and demand to know what he had been doing. He was astonished and touched by their welcome.

"I was sent to Dunfaol to fetch the Lord of the Isles," he said. "How goes the war here?"

They all began talking at once. He soon learned that his success had been even more vital than he had realized. There would almost certainly be a big battle the very next day. Refusing to be distracted by Constantine's attack on Lothian on the east coast, King Osian had brought a large army against Malcolm's, pinning it there against the shore. The Albans were outnumbered and could not evacuate by sea, because loading the entire army into the ships would drastically overload them, rendering them helpless against any bad weather, or an attack by the Osian's navy. Now there was no need to run, because Thorfinn's reinforcements should turn the odds in Alba's favour.

But then the other runners wanted to know how Ivor had managed to recruit all those Northmen to fight on God's side—and that was where the conversation grew tricky. He *really* did not want to be branded with the reputation of working miracles. He hummed and he hawed. And still they sat there, six bright eyes firmly fixed on him, and they weren't going to let him escape until he told all. He was forbidden to discuss any message he carried, even with other members of the team, but events were public, and the Dunfaol story was certainly going to come out.

"Well, um," he said. "It's a strange business. I had a lot of help from Saint Seumas."

"Who?"

He began to tell them about the strange blessing he had received on Eyin Helga, but then he was reprieved, at least for a short while. A stranger dressed like a Northman, complete with gold rings on his arms and a battle-axe hung on his back, was striding between tents, heading in the group's direction. Galan nudged Ivor to remind him that he was now spokesman.

He jumped up and bowed. "I am captain of runners, my lord. How can I be of service?" He guessed then that this could only be Snorri Ragnvaldson. He looked very little older than Ivor himself, and his expression suggested that he had guessed what news he was about to hear.

"I understand that one of your men has just returned from the Isles, from Dunfaol?"

"That was me, my lord, Ivor of Glenbroch." Ivor felt sorry for him. Whether he had been sent south to a strange land as a hostage or as a refugee, his plight was about to become even worse.

"You?" But he did not follow up with a comment on Ivor's youth. "Earl Ragnvaldr has been deposed?"

Ivor nodded. "On the day we arrived, my lord, but before we got there, so I only know at secondhand what happened. I deeply regret to tell you that both your father and Erik your brother were slain, and the bishop also, but no others that I know of. Thane Thorfinn Fleinn arrived with a fleet, and many more ships came in later. The thanes all hailed him as…as their leader. I am sorry to have to give you such dread news."

Snorri nodded sadly. "Any word of my mother and sisters?"

"None that I heard, my lord." Bloodcurdling stories had been passed around on *Dragonfire* but Ivor was not going to repeat those. "My lord, am I right in thinking that your honoured father expected this to happen?"

The Northmen frowned. "Not at all. He thought he had dealt with Thorfinn."

It was Ivor's turn to be surprised. "I thought it was on your warning that Mormaor Malcolm decided at the last minute to send me north."

Snorri shook his head. "He told me he had had a bad dream about it and asked me if it might be a true vision."

So Ivor had been sent into harm's way by a dream? Clearly he was not the only one who had been granted miracles, and God had spared Alba.

For a moment Snorri just stared into the distance as if he had forgotten Ivor and the watchers. Then he brought his mind back to the present and squared his shoulders. "They say the King of Dublin needs warriors." He reached in his pouch for a coin.

Ivor said. "That is kind of you, my lord, but I cannot accept it."

Snorri nodded, turned, and walked away. Ivor sat down.

"Why not?" asked Ilgarach. "That was *silver* he was going to give you!"

"I only accept gifts from Malcolm," Ivor said. *"And so do you!"*

Ilgarach flinched as if Ivor had struck him. Three voices loudly agreed.

Authority was very strong beer.

"Or the king, of course," Ivor added, remembering his ring.

▶▼◀

He was summoned to Malcolm's tent just after sunset. Thorfinn was there too, and the pair of them had obviously been drinking together for some time, pretending to be friends. Their matching thrones had been improvised from packs and boxes.

"Captain of Runners," Malcolm said, and paused as if he had forgotten why he had sent for him. "I'm told you work miracles now?"

"Saint Seumas sent a miracle for us, my lord. I only followed the instructions the holy man gave me on Eyin Helga."

"Mm." Malcolm looked skeptical. "I'll hear it all tomorrow after the battle."

"After the victory, my lord!"

"Hope so. Post two runners with me, two with Earl Thorfinn, so we can commumm...umminicate." He burped and took a drink. "On horses. Unarmed! A runner's job is to stay *out* of the fighting, remember."

That seemed to be all, so Ivor saluted and departed.

▶▼◀

Horses? How did you requisition horses in an army camp on the eve of a major battle? How was he supposed to learn all this? He needed Ninian to teach... But Ninian must be here, somewhere. He was quartermaster now.

The first man he asked directed him to the commissary, and there was Ninian, checking the unloading of a wagonload of grain sacks by lantern light, counting on an abacus.

"Ninian!"

Ninian looked up with delight. "Ivor! The hero!" He thumped Ivor's shoulder with his free hand, the one lacking a thumb. "The man who works miracles!"

"Never mind miracles! Or rather, you must do one now. You have to teach me how to be captain of runners because we've got a battle coming and I don't know spit. So teach me everything. You have ten minutes!"

Ninian was grinning. "I don't have to. You obviously know how to do it already."

"Huh?"

"You speak with the mormaor's voice, lad. You don't ask, you just give orders, like the one you just gave me, and no one will question whose orders they are, unless you ask for something utterly stupid. Just look confident. That's the secret and all the secret. Don't shout. Speak low and look menacing."

"I can't look menacing!"

"Oh yes you can! Those dark eyes and thick eyebrows of yours give you a very good glare."

Not sure how much he was having his leg pulled, but remembering how he had spooked Ilgarach, Ivor shrugged and said. "Oh! Right. Thank you."

"Now tell me about the miracle at Dunfaol."

"Can't. No time. *Get back to work, Ninian of Whisht!*"

Then they both laughed, and Ivor asked him the way to the master of horse.

▶▼◀

He slept badly that night. When he did drop off, it seemed only minutes before drums began beating the reveille.

The battle was a disappointment, although definitely a great victory. He chose himself and Edan to ride out to the Northmen's camp, and left the others to attend Malcolm.

The Alban strategy was very simple, but worked very well. Osian and Malcolm lined up their opposing forces on a swampy, flat field, and for a while just shouted insults at one another. Thorfinn led his army around behind some low dunes to the south, and then made everyone sit down and be quiet. Nothing much happened for an hour that felt like a week. Then they began to hear drums, shouts, bugles, and screams, all of them sounding very far away.

Eventually Galan came into view on a foam-flecked horse, waving his arms before he was close enough to shout. The men of the Isles surged to their feet and Thorfinn led them stumbling and cursing over the soft sand of the dunes. Ivor and Edan followed on horseback.

The noise at once grew much louder, and Ivor was surprised to see how close the battle actually was. The Northumbrians had been winning, driving the Albans back, but their triumph turned to panic when another army came charging in on their flank. Fascinated, horrified, and both happy and ashamed to be out of it, Ivor stayed back and kept his eyes on Thorfinn. Whatever else you might say about the man, he fought like a rabid bear. Soon the Northumbrian wall broke and after that it was butchery.

Chapter 11

***"Malcolm of Stiegle,** Mormaor of the West, and Thorfinn Fleinn of Dunfaol, Mormaor of the Isles, together send loyal greetings to their liege lord, Constantine, King of the Scots and Picts, Lord of Alba, saying: today we fought shoulder to shoulder at Nilcaster in the name of Christ Our Lord, who sent us great victory; we made wondrous slaughter of the Northumbrians and took captive Osian their king, who throws himself upon your mercy and asks your terms for peace. Thus spake Malcolm and Thorfinn."*

It was the same tent as the night before, but with the addition of some candles, because Ivor had not been summoned until a later hour. There was also a lesser makeshift throne for the defeated King Osian, who had a bandage around his head where his crown should be, and looked utterly crushed. He was going to lose Lothian and perhaps other lands also. Kings who lost battles might lose everything. The two earls were almost sober, because the beer had run out. The rest of the camp was making up for it with singing, trying to drown out the screams of the dying and wounded as gashes were sewn up and arrowheads extracted; also the sound of shovels, picks, and whips as the prisoners dug graves.

"That's it," Malcolm added after dictating the message. "Uvan son of Hamish can give you a list of dead and wounded thanes and tanists. Detail two runners to take it to the king, by separate routes. A four man escort for each—all on horseback, of course. And one runner to take the news by sea to Stiegle."

Ivor said, "Aye, my lord. We'll leave at dawn."

Malcolm smiled. "And you'll send yourself by sea?"

"Aye, my lord." He had earned this much!

"Which ship do you want?"

"*Sea Eagle*, if it's seaworthy." He didn't know yet how many of his brothers had fallen in the battle.

Malcolm nodded. On the way to Stiegle the ship would certainly need to fill its water casks at Glenbroch, and would probably overnight there.

Thorfinn spoke up. "Runner Ivor, I'll pay you a silver shilling a month to come and serve me, plus a house of your own, and as many beautiful girl serfs as you need."

Ivor bowed and decided that the hero of the hour could risk some humour. "I don't think I'm old enough for even one beautiful serf, my lord, but ask me again when Earl Malcolm isn't around."

They both laughed, and Malcolm roared, "Out, you ungrateful scoundrel!"

Ivor found Uvan son of Hamish, who was Malcolm's chief clerk. Uvan offered to write out the names of the important dead for him, but Ivor insisted that just reading the list to him would be enough. Then he went back to the runners' tent and passed on that information and the mormaors' message to Galan and Gest, who were both known at court.

After that he found Housecarl Uvan son of Domlech and told him he would need eight swordsmen and ten mounts at first light. He didn't win a salute, but he didn't get any argument, either—he was starting to enjoy this strange secondhand authority he had been given. As he went past the commissariat, he saw Ninian supervising a team that was sorting out a huge heap of confiscated weapons and armour. Being a runner was a better job.

He had a longer walk to find *Sea Eagle*, but even when he told them they would be heading home on the morrow, there was little rejoicing there. Two of the crew had died, one of them being Fergus of Bracken, brother Number Seven. But Thane Tasgall Mór was also among the dead, making Tanist Angus now thane of Glenbroch. The hird had already met and elected Big Dermid as the new tanist, and *Sea Eagle* was traditionally the tanist's ship. So Angus must remain behind to lead the rest of the Glenbroch contingent, but as thane he could assign any three of those men to bring *Sea Eagle* up to strength and send it on its way.

▶▼◀

It sailed when dawn was breaking, with Ivor aboard as cargo and water boy. Sitting on the bench beside Dermid, listening to the tap of the mallet and the creak of the oars, with the sea wind rippling his hair, he thought about Glenbroch, which he had always considered home, but had not seen for three months. He was taking both good and bad news with him, news of victory and news of bereavements. Neither Tasgall nor Fergus had been married, but all the other Glenbroch dead had left families. He had no doubts what his reception would be—by the time Jock, Lachlan, and Tomas had finished embroidering the story, he would have personally worked miracles at Dunfaol and singlehandedly saved Malcolm from certain defeat at Nilcaster. And he couldn't deny that that wasn't far from the truth. Glenbroch mothers would be naming babies after him for years.

Stiegle felt more like home now. There he would have to recite the entire litany of the dead, for Dermid could not be expected to remember the names of scores of strangers, but in Stiegle rejoicing at the mormaor's triumph would outweigh the sorrow.

What of Lady Meg? On the day he had been sent north, he had confirmed for her that her future husband was not about to arrive in *Sea Eagle*. He had thought then that she seemed more relieved than disappointed. Now he must break the news that Tasgall would never come. How would she react to that? Would she shun the raven that croaked ill tidings? Was it remotely possible that she would look with admiration and approval on the hero of Dunfaol?

He had been granted one miracle. To hope for another would be greedy.

Reality Check

Alba is the Gaelic name for Scotland. King Constantine II ruled Alba from 900 to 943, but it did not grow to its present size until several centuries later, and little is known about those far-off days. In England and most of Europe, honours came from above—the kings named the lords—but in Scotland power came from below. How important you were depended on how many armed men would follow you.

About the Author

Originally from Scotland, Dave Duncan has lived all his adult life in Western Canada, having enjoyed a long career as a petroleum geologist before taking up writing. Since discovering that imaginary worlds are more satisfying than the real one, he has published more than forty-five novels, mostly in the fantasy genre, but also young adult, science fiction, and historical. He has at times been Sarah B. Franklin (but only for literary purposes) and Ken Hood (which is short for "D'ye Ken Whodunit?")

His most successful works have been fantasy series: The Seventh Sword, A Man of His Word and its sequel, A Handful of Men, and six books about The King's Blades.

He and Janet were married in 1959. They have one son and two daughters, who in turn are responsible for a spinoff series of four grandchildren. Dave now lives in Victoria, BC.

A detailed discussion of his work from Gale's "Dictionary of Literary Biography" is available for download from Amazon.com.

Books by Five Rivers

NON-FICTION

Al Capone: Chicago's King of Crime, by Nate Hendley

Crystal Death: North America's Most Dangerous Drug, by Nate Hendley

Dutch Schultz: Brazen Beer Baron of New York, by Nate Hendley

Motivate to Create: a guide for writers, by Nate Hendley

The Organic Home Gardener, by Patrick Lima and John Scanlan

Elephant's Breath & London Smoke: historic colour names, definitions & uses, Deb Salisbury, editor

Stonehouse Cooks, by Lorina Stephens

John Lennon: a biography, by Nate Hendley

Shakespeare & Readers' Theatre: Hamlet, Romeo & Juliet, Midsummer Night's Dream, by John Poulson

Stephen Truscott, by Nate Hendley

FICTION

Black Wine, by Candas Jane Dorsey

88, by M.E. Fletcher

Immunity to Strange Tales, by Susan J. Forest

The Legend of Sarah, by Leslie Gadallah

Growing Up Bronx, by H.A. Hargreaves

North by 2000+, a collection of short, speculative fiction, by H.A. Hargreaves

A Subtle Thing, Alicia Hendley

Downshift, by Matt Hughes

Old Growth, by Matt Hughes

Kingmaker's Sword, Book 1: Rune Blades of Celi, by Ann Marston

Western King, Book 2: The Rune Blades of Celi, by Ann Marston

Broken Blade, Book 3: The Rune Blades of Celi, by Ann Marston

Cloudbearer's Shadow, Book 4: The Rune Blades of Celi, by Ann Marston
Indigo Time, by Sally McBride
Wasps at the Speed of Sound, by Derryl Murphy
A Method to Madness: A Guide to the Super Evil, edited by Michell Plested and Jeffery A. Hite
A Quiet Place, by J.W. Schnarr
Things Falling Apart, by J.W. Schnarr
And the Angels Sang: a collection of short speculative fiction, by Lorina Stephens
From Mountains of Ice, by Lorina Stephens
Memories, Mother and a Christmas Addiction, by Lorina Stephens
Shadow Song, by Lorina Stephens

YA FICTION

The Runner and the Wizard, by Dave Duncan
The Runner and the Saint, by Dave Duncan
Out of Time, by D.G. Laderoute
Mik Murdoch: Boy-Superhero, by Michell Plested
Type, by Alicia Hendley

FICTION COMING SOON

Kaleidoscope, by Robert Fletcher
Cat's Pawn, by Leslie Gadallah
Cat's Gambit, by Leslie Gadallah
King of Shadows, Book 5: The Rune Blades of Celi, by Ann Marston
Sword and Shadow, Book 6: The Rune Blades of Celi, by Ann Marston
Bane's Choice, Book 7: The Rune Blades of Celi, by Ann Marston
A Still and Bitter Grave, by Ann Marston
Diamonds in Black Sand, by Ann Marston
Forevering, by Peter Such

YA FICTION COMING SOON

My Life as a Troll, by Susan Bohnet

A Touch of Poison, by Aaron Kite
Mik Murdoch: The Power Within, by Michell Plested

YA NON-FICTION COMING SOON

Your Home on Native Land, by Alan Skeoch
The Prime Ministers of Canada Series:
  Sir John A. Macdonald
  Alexander Mackenzie
  Sir John Abbott
  Sir John Thompson
  Sir Mackenzie Bowell
  Sir Charles Tupper
  Sir Wilfred Laurier
  Sir Robert Borden
  Arthur Meighen
  William Lyon Mackenzie King
  R. B. Bennett
  Louis St. Laurent
  John Diefenbaker
  Lester B. Pearson
  Pierre Trudeau
  Joe Clark
  John Turner
  Brian Mulroney
  Kim Campbell
  Jean Chretien
  Paul Martin
  Stephen Harper

www.fiveriverspublishing.com

The Runner and the Wizard

by Dave Duncan

ISBN 9781927400395 $11.99

eISBN 9781927400401 $4.99

Trade Paperback 6 x 9, 100 pages

October 1, 2013

Young Ivor dreams of being a swordsman like his nine older brothers, but until he can grow a beard he's limited to being a runner, carrying messages for their lord, Thane Carrak. That's usually boring, but this time Carrak has sent him on a long journey to summon the mysterious Rorie of Ytter. Rorie is reputed to be a wizard—or an outlaw, or maybe a saint—but the truth is far stranger, and Ivor suddenly finds himself caught up in a twisted magical intrigue that threatens Thane Carrak and could leave Ivor himself very dead.

Kingmaker's Sword, Book 1, The Rune Blades of Celi

by Ann Marston

ISBN 9781927400166 $37.99

eISBN 9781927400173 $9.99

Trade Paperback 6 x 9, 504 pages

August 1, 2012

Triumphing over adversity and evil, Kian dav Leydon brings the fabled Rune Blade Kingmaker back to the Isle of Celi after it was stolen, so the Isle will be ready when and if invasion comes.

A re-print of Ann Marston's Book 1 of the much beloved Rune Blades of Celi series.

Indigo Time

by Sally McBride

ISBN 9781927400319 $24.99

eISBN 9781927400326 $4.99

Trade paperback 6 x 9, 302 pages

August 1, 2013

Marrula Tamara, once Empress of Worlds, has been exiled for treachery to a planet called Strand. She has one great treasure: the engineered horse Raj'azul. In his blood lies the secret of her immortality…and the seed of her downfall.

From Mountains of Ice

by Lorina Stephens

ISBN 9780973927856 $23.99

eISBN 9780986563027 $4.99

Trade Paperback 6 x 9, 268 pages

September 1, 2009

Sylvio spent the past decade banished from Simare's court, stripped of land, ancestral home and title - from Minister of National Security to back-country bowyer. But not any bowyer; Sylvio creates bows from laminations of wood and human bone, bows that are said to speak, bows known as the legendary arcossi.

And now, after a decade, he is called back to the capitol, summoned by his Prince whom he suspects is a patricide and insane. His very life is in danger and with it the country he has served through all his days.